RACHEL'S SONG

a novel by
Miguel Barnet

translated by
W. Nick Hill

CURBSTONE PRESS

Cover design by Modesto Braulio
Printed in the U.S. by BookCrafters

This publication was supported in part by donations, and by
grants from The National Endowment for the Arts and The
Connecticut Commission on the Arts, a state agency whose
funds are recommended by the Governor and appropriated
by the State Legislature.

The translator gratefully acknowledges the generous
assistance of The Center for Cuban Studies, especially
Rachel, and Gilberto B., John Coleman, Javier Campos, Alan
West, Sandy Taylor, Judy Doyle, and my best reader, Barbara
Arnn.

ISBN: 0-915306-87-5
Library of Congress number: 91-55412

distributed by
InBook
Box 120470
East Haven, CT 06512

published by
CURBSTONE PRESS
321 Jackson Street
Willimantic, CT 06226

How small the world is in the eyes of memory.
— Baudelaire

Rachel's confessions, her troubled life during the scintillating years of the Cuban belle epoque, conversations in the cafes, in the streets, have made possible a book which reflects the frustrated atmosphere of republican life. Rachel was a sui generis witness. She represents the age. She is somewhat of a synthesis of all the show girls who appeared at the defunct Alhambra Theater, a true gauge of the country's social and political activities. The characters who appear in the book, and who complement the central monologue, are by and large men of the theater, writers, lyricists, and inevitably, the ones behind the scenes. Rachel's Song speaks of the person, of her life, as she told it to me and as I then told it for her.

— Miguel Barnet

RACHEL'S SONG

Chapter One

This island is something special. The strangest, most tragic things have happened here. And it will always be that way. The earth, like human kind, has its destiny. And Cuba's is a mysterious destiny. I'm not a witch, or a reader of cards or anything like that. I don't know how to read palms the way one should, but I've always said to myself that whoever is born on this piece of ground has his mission, for good or ill. Things don't happen here like in other places where loads of people are all born the same, behave the same, and live and die anonymously. No. Whoever is born in Cuba has his star assured, or his cross, because there are also those who are born to bang their heads against the wall.

Now, what you call a milquetoast, who's not either one thing or another, a ninny, you don't see that type here.

This island is predestined for the divine commandments to be obeyed here. For that reason I've always looked on it with respect. I've tried to live on it the best way I can, caring for it and keeping myself as center. For that, the best thing is to work, to entertain yourself with something and don't give free rein to your mind because that's the worst. Cuba is my home. I was born here and I became a woman and an entertainer here. And here is where I want to die, because if there's a place I'd like to be buried it's in this little spot. I've seen other countries, all very beautiful, very modern and very courteous, with very cordial people, but with the warmth of my homeland, not one. And I'm even of European descent. My mother was Hungarian and my father, German. She Hungarian and he German. She, short and freckled, very fun loving. A little lady with backbone. My father, I don't have any idea. I saw him, I used to see him every time Mama would show me his photograph. He seemed like a good looking young man. At least in that portrait.

"He was German, little one," my mother would say. "You got that hard little head of yours from him."

My mother provided me with a good education. And above all, much love for your neighbor. She had this genuine gift of convincing you, and convince she did. Mama loved humanity. She spoke well of everyone so that they'd respect her. And she never got entangled with anyone. Not even with married men. On the contrary, she avoided marriage. I was her reason for being, the first and only thing in her life.

Mama's friends would come up to the house. And me: "Hello, how are you?" and that was that, because as soon as one of them arrived, the little girl goes straight to her room to play and she's real careful not to stick even the tip of her nose out the door.

Mother knew how to be stern and sweet at the same time. There was no god who would disobey her. Even the servant girl was afraid of her. A servant who was more than that, a friend, a companion, and, still, everything was: "You called, Madame, Ma'am, please, Excuse me, Ma'am, If Madame wishes," and what not, so I, who was her daughter, her own blood, had to live terrified in spite of the fact that Mama was my only love, the only person I had in the world.

Sometimes I dreamed Mama came and wrapped me up in a quilt and we two would sleep together. I was happy in that dream. Other times Mama would take up the whole bed and I'd fall on the floor. Kaboom! Then I'd wake up and nothing had happened, because I would be sleeping alone, all alone. My habit of always sleeping with a little light on comes from those years.

The devil things are, because old as I am, as peaceful and mature, I haven't been able to put a stop to it.

Mother did everything for me. She sacrificed her life to give me a respectable career and she succeeded.

I live in the alleyway. What I know about Rachel is what there was between the two of us, and that's personal.

Better if we cross that bridge some other day. Not today, she's sick with the flu now. Just let her be. She died with the theater, she was left behind, and she has nothing to say about any of it.

Allow her to remain in her Parnassus, if you remove her, then certainly Rachel is no more.

In any case, tomorrow I'll let her know about some of this. We'll see what she says. She pays attention to me. We were husband and wife and now it happens that by chance I live two steps from her house.

Thirty five years without seeing her. Life is like that!

There are those of us who come into the world with just such an attraction. I believe that whatever destiny holds in store for you always comes about.

That's what I was telling her the other day: "Gal, you and I are like they say in the song: prisoners in the same cell."

Mama was not what you'd call a floozy, a loose woman.

Whoever talks like that is mistaken. My mother had her life, she lived it her way, she did with her body whatever she pleased. Walking a tightrope to survive and plenty of courage. That was my mother.

To tell the truth, I can't complain about her. I guess my native sense made me understand her all the way down to the particulars. She knew that even as a little girl, I had sniffed it out, but she never spoke of it openly. She was always slippery about that. She'd get away from me along the edges.

And since I was already smart, I kept quiet. Who better than from my mother was I going to hide her affairs, her secrets. There's not much that I could really say about my mother. It's not because she's under the ground and that we have to be respectful, no. It's more because she was like a saint with me, she devoted herself to my whims, to my foolishness. I'd ask for a bird on the wing and off my mother would go to bring a bird on the wing.

Talking about her makes me sad, but it clears my mind. When you love that way, it's good to constantly talk about the other person because then the love grows.

There are days when I get to talking about my mother and I go on without stopping.

Then days go by when I don't think about her. At night is when I think about her most. At night, Ofelia leaves and I lie down on the bed with those white pillows.

Ofelia is a great companion, she takes care of me, she puts up with what no one else does, but it's not the same as a mother. For Mama I was always the silly, the absent-minded one, the doll.

I am alone, yes, alone. But I'm not a woman who makes a mountain out of a molehill. I'm not hysterical either. Dramatic, even less. The word wretch I never apply to myself. I'm a sad, melancholy person.

Listen to that. What is that woman thinking of. If they let her have her way, if they let her . . .

She wasn't born with any silver spoon in her mouth, and that's not the way she's gone. She was brought up pretty poor, with a lot of twisting around by her mother, and a lot of hunger. I know because I was acquainted with the family. She always was quite self-centered. You pass by and see her dolled up and all, but to say she was raised from the cradle like that is really stretching it.

Rachel was born in a neighborhood whose name it's better not to even mention. Knifings, depravity, robbery.

She came out pretty clean.

She was never anything but a rumba dancer. The only thing she knew how to do was wiggle.

She wiggled all her life. She's ignorant, wild, and frivolous.

A frivolous woman and nothing more. No, I don't like to talk about her.

The loveliest thing is to look back with happiness. To see yourself like in a movie, as a playful child, just sitting straight up in an armchair, playing the piano . . . I love that.

We were what has come to be called middle class. Not rich not poor.

Havana was beginning to take off, to become a city of progress, inspiring real admiration. The electric trolley was one of the big happenings. People stopped on the street, when I was a girl, and looked with their eyes wide, they were dazed watching it move pushed by electricity.

After the initial slight fear of getting on, they would ride it every day just for pleasure.

What I know well is that part of San Isidro, the neighborhood around the Train Terminal, the old city wall. That's the Havana of my youth: very pretty and lively.

We lived in a boarding house, in a cramped room that did have some ventilation. Mama wasn't fond of moving like a Gypsy. She preferred staying in one place. To move is to change mood and that was upsetting to her, since we were alone and she was a foreigner and all, with her own brand of Cubanness . . .

By nine I was already playing piano some and dancing rumbas. It was in my nature.

In school I always stood out above the others. They called me the star. And I believed it. In all the shows I danced or played my little number or recited. I always did it well. From then on, from the time I was a girl, I've pleased people. I got the habit of that little world of applause and "great, how cute, what a little figure" and when I first came to see theater, I was already inoculated with the fatal virus of performing.

I wasn't able to get rid of it. I pestered people to death everywhere trying get them to do something for my art. I worked at becoming a headliner, and with my mother's help I succeeded. A guy named Rolen was the first to get me on stage. I was probably about 13 and had left school because hunger was at the door and Mama was wary. This guy Rolen would come and take me, always at the side of my dear mother, to a theater that used to be in Cerro. We would sit there, the three of us. Rolen, my old lady and me. The show was like a cheap circus where two or three young girls danced showing off for the young men in the first row. A very decent kind of language, certainly, no vulgar talk or talking tough.

I looked up at the ceiling like a fool because I felt sorry for the girls. My eyes would just go up and this Rolen guy would take my head and lower it, obliging me to watch them.

He was a nice man who wanted to help both of us. And it seems he had stock in it or a lot of influence, because three weeks later I was dancing at the Tivoli, in the afternoon show, as a chorus girl.

My body was right and I was good at hearing the music. I was never off key when I started a song. I never fell, never made a big mistake, and I never forgot a single step.

I knew that stage like the back of my hand after a few weeks. So much so that I flowered right away, getting the swing of it, and of course, I was the first dancer of the company. Thirteen or fourteen, but with a woman's body. Once in awhile my elementary school teachers called me to do my little piece at school and I'd go. I did a little girl, a Galician maiden, an opera singer intoning arias. A bit of everything!

One day one of them found out, I don't know from whom, that I was a professional, and she went to my house to raise a ruckus with my mother. She felt an obligation to do it. Those

14

pious women in high collars were old fashioned and my mother wasn't. Mama had a practical, modern sense of life.

Well, the teacher goes and begins with the I'll have you know this and you should know that. And the only memory I have of it is that my mother drummed her out of the house with insults. She did the right thing because I was of sound mind, and everything I did was of my own free will. Dancing young isn't bad. The bad thing is to use dancing as a way to do business. But there was no one who could make that old thing understand. Besides which, she wasn't going to pay for the electricity, or the rent.

Since then I've always felt a great respect for the performer who's been in a tight spot. Nor have I been one of those censors of public evil, dressed in black, those Catholic ladies, those . . .

Never have I wanted to take away anyone's fantasy. Because a fantasy realized is worth anything. If you don't think so, just ask me about it, because I did in life what my fantasy wished, from childhood on.

Before starting at the Tivoli I was a naive little girl, a Catholic schoolgirl.

I was cured of a lot of things there. I opened my eyes to the world.

I used to arrive in the afternoon, rehearse a little, leave, grab a bite and then, on to the show. Mama in back of me the entire time. I think she was afraid they would rape me or mistreat me.

I began to buy clothes: lamé, silks, *guaracha* dresses, evening gowns.

I put together a pretty coquettish wardrobe that was more or less dignified.

How afraid my old lady was that her daughter might turn out bad! Once when I was singing a ditty, I don't remember which, a young man yells at me: "Jump, doll!"

I was puzzled by that jump. What did it mean? I make a negative sign. So he lunges forward and grabs my legs in the middle of the number. I punched him in the nose right in front of the audience and they closed the curtains. Since all performers tell the story of their first incident, that was mine. And he was my first lover.

Even now I'm surprised looking back and reading the letters, not the letters, the joy, the news my prince sent to me.

What a strange feeling, anybody would say I'm crazy: in that trunk is the residue of those years, 1902, 1903, 1904, 1906 . . . (Magoon, yes, it was Magoon.)

14 July, 1906

What you most resemble is a rose. Let this stand as a declaration of love.

Eusebio

The Tivoli was a cheap theater that had been built in Palatino. Year of 1906, if I remember right. I went often. In those days we men had to entertain ourselves with that kind of thing. I was always much given to women. Rachel began there as a chorus girl, a bad one. She danced, still a girl, on holidays and then during her free time she'd rest, all covered up, of course. She got together some money there and left. How did she get to the Alhambra? I don't know. A woman could get to the Alhambra for any number of reasons. Rachel arrived, that's sure. And she blossomed, so to speak, she got ahead and came out on top.

She did her act at the end of each show. The acts meant you wiggled your ass at the close of the performance every night. They'd play a very elegant danzón and you'd fold your arms to listen in absolute silence, then they'd put on the play and close with a drum rumba Rachel did, the only female dancer. She did it as a duo with a guy named Pepe.

Her fame spread like wildfire. All the men wanted her but me. I like truly cultivated women and hers was a poor finish, bargain basement quality.

16

It's said, vox populi, that one night the great Spanish classical writer and man of orthodox letters don Jacinto Benavente arrived for a performance at the Alhambra Theater, and it seems that the old man enjoyed it because he went back to the dressing rooms and sent flowers to all the principal figures. Many Japanese daisies for Rachel and many kisses, as is customary between writers and show girls.

She, playing the generous one, and she was, and not badly trained, no, on the contrary, she lived for details . . . Well, she offers the old man a drink, he takes it and then a dialogue begins you could die from.

"You are a very attractive woman."

"And you a gentlemen who spoils ladies."

"I would like you to visit Castile and go to Cataluña to perform."

"I am very grateful, don Jacinto, but where I want to go is Europe."

The old man catches on and changes the topic.

"Rachel, do you like the opera?"

"Yes, of course, and I always dreamed of being a soprano, but, there you are."

"Which opera do you like?"

"All of them, don Jacinto, all of them."

"Well, look, I'll stick with Andrea Chénier. Have you heard it, Rachel?"

"Yes, do you mean the first soprano?"

And such were the things that happened to that young woman, because later she travelled and polished herself quite a bit. But returning to the woman, to be honest, I preferred Luz.

Eusebio gave me a lot of headaches. I was pretty young for that kind of social whirl. But he didn't take heed. He was constantly on my trail. If I moved, he moved. I'd sit, he'd sit. He was sticky sweet like that.

I got used to loving like a silly. My mother gave up on us as incurable and let us have our great adventure by ourselves.

That's how the only pure love of my life began.

His family was opposed to us. They had shoe factories, sugar mills and a bunch of other things. I wasn't thinking of all that. He was the one who interested me. But they thought something else. And they made my life, our life, impossible: that period was a vale of tears for me.

Eusebio didn't miss a day's performance. All to see me, of course. He'd bring me gifts, he spoiled me, he was my dream.

One day there was a fire in the theater and I was nearly burned all the way up to my hair.

Eusebio was furious because he'd already been going on with the litany that I had to leave that place, and he took me away for a few days, without my mother's consent. All under wraps. Instead of going to the theater, we went to the beaches, Chivo and others, and we'd do whatever we wanted in the sand, in the ocean itself.

We lived a real debauch. The two of us were happy by ourselves. But Mama finds out and puts up a real fuss. So to please her, I return to the theater.

Eusebio understood the problem and it wasn't on that account that he stopped seeing me. On the contrary, he became even crazier about me. But no marriage. His parents opposed it to the bitter end.

25 November, 1906

My love,

These days without you have no meaning for me. I don't ask you to write because I know the letters won't reach me. Our distance unites me to you. I despair.

Eusebio

They would send him out into the country, to check on money matters and other business. They isolated him from me. I couldn't write to him because I didn't know where to. I didn't have messengers or third parties. Nothing. I was at a complete disadvantage. In a pit.

I lost my desire to work. Things began to come out backwards. The Tivoli didn't fill up for me. I lived trapped in my feelings for that man, isolated from myself. I spent day and night thinking of him. And all my thoughts I kept to myself, they were officially mine. None of those little stories to other girls, no white lies. That love was mine and everything that had to do with it I reserved for myself.

I've never liked gossipy women, the bragging kind. That type doesn't have any consideration. They don't love anybody. They announce their lovers as if they were merchandise, and they tell each other all the details from A to Z.

To my mind that is a woman's worst sin.

Eusebio . . . his story, was his and mine. Nobody else had anything to do with it. At least when it comes to the inner matters, because since it was a tragic, public story people knew more than they should, unfortunately, unfortunately.

The papers reported all the lurid details. Photographs and interviews.

They didn't touch me. I don't know, I hid myself away in someone's house.

The whole city was astir with the suicide, and affluent families, the Casanovas, the Marqueses by Royal Proclamation, the Montalvos, distanced themselves from Eusebio's family, from his mother and father. That's the aristocracy. Everything inside and when something is uncovered, run and cover it up. It's a falsity you can't even name.

I don't remember the date when Eusebio committed suicide. The year was probably '07 or the beginning of '08. The little details like the day and the hour, I just can't.

I was so horrified that I lost my memory and my ability to talk. And no one sympathized with me. Just the opposite, they thought I was to blame. Even my own mother, after putting up with our foolishness for so long, rubbed my nose in it. Her inconsistencies!

We'd gone in the afternoon to the baths. Carneado Beaches they were called. Delightful hot pools, where everyone went who wanted it like that. Provided we could slip away, we used to go there all the time. Afterwards, we'd go out and drink beer and dance.

Some shrill but fun orchestras played at those beaches.

Since I was a professional dancer, Eusebio held himself back and didn't dance the way a man should who wanted to please a girl. He'd get stiff, really strange, and look all around. The typical bashful dancer, the timid one.

When the sun set, we'd leave. My boyfriend had a red Rolls Royce, a convertible. It had cost him twenty-four thousand dollars in Paris.

He asked me if I loved him. And I told him yes, I loved him. Then he started to give me hot kisses. He bit me, he hugged me. I thought it was strange but I didn't want to cool him down, and he kept on and on.

All real good till we got to my house.

We got out of the car and he walked me to the door.

In the doorway he told me the whole story. The Asturian woman who had a room in the attic of my house had made the place available so he and I could stay there until midnight. That woman was something else, a friend of Mama's and a kind of godmother to me. But I didn't play the fool, or act surprised.

I went because I was in love with my boyfriend and because other times we had spent hours and hours together in the same bed. I remembered it all. Those moments when a whole history of things pass through your mind. But I rose above it and said to myself: "You're a complete woman and you're in love, don't be afraid." Eusebio didn't do a thing but repeat: "Age doesn't matter, sweetie. Love doesn't go around looking at that. Today I want you to be mine."

He softened me up completely. I felt different. Now it wasn't just a matter of playing.

Desire burned in me.

It was the happiest night of my life because I gave myself to love.

Eusebio took my virginity, blood and all. I cried freely, took a bath, and we left, both of us scared to death.

The Asturian woman was waiting for us downstairs. I covered my face with a hand towel, out of shame and because she was one the of the ugliest bugs that ever crawled the earth. She had yellow hair and some long whiskers on her chin. Not a breath of it to Mama.

With all this, the Tivoli robbed me of more time every day. A woman of my caliber was prized like gold.

Eusebio and I kept on. More love every day, more kisses, more . . .

Until one night some spots begin to appear on my skin, and nausea. When I told him I was pregnant he squeezed me and congratulated me.

And he went to tell his dear mother. That dog put on a face that not even the devil . . . and he came back to me disconsolate. That's when the drama began. His mother saying no, no and he saying yes, and me too.

Mama, as far as I was able, remained more or less in the dark.

After two or three months they took me to a doctor. I aborted a sixth-month-old boy. My placenta stuck inside and the doctor had to take it out piece by piece. Those were bitter hours in my existence.

I kept on dancing. Now in the night show. And he hid himself away or they hid him. That woman was a demon in mother's clothing. A few days after my abortion, the photograph appeared in La Discusión. Eusebio had moved to a house his brother had, a love nest, and there, one afternoon, in front of a mirror, he slit his throat. It happened on Estrada Palma Street, in the Jesús del Monte section.

Instead of killing himself with a rifle or a shotgun, he chose a kitchen knife and used that. His brother had a small gun room for hanging game birds and he had hidden all the weapons.

He later declared that Eusebio had told him he would carry out that rash act if they didn't let him see his wife, me.

I never went down that street again. My life was ripped to shreds. My name in the dirt, and his prestige likewise, since he was high class, a member of the Yacht Club. Between the two of us it was a Greek tragedy.

The only thing that remained of it all was a sealed letter where Eusebio said:

Rach: I love you.

I have Mariana Grajales stuck up on the armoire and I pray to her. That woman was the mother of Cuba. A true saint. America's Joan of Arc. Oh, Marianita, keep him in glory and take care of my country!

That's a summary of my life, which is very sad.

She ended up hoarse on account of some messy problem she was having. Really, really hoarse. The owner couldn't make her keep on singing. So she perfected the dancing part she already knew and the storm passed by.

I never talked to the stars there. A ticket-taker didn't get close to the performers. I like individuality. Rachel seemed pretty decent. All of them there were young girls who earned their living by shaking their behinds, but they were okay and friendly. The real show was outside, after the last performance. The Tivoli gives me the creeps. While there I caught yellow fever and was saved by a miracle.

22

Hands are the mirror of the soul. They taught me all that a performer needs to learn. Hands one manages well, with grace and ease, do half the work. My hands were a charm. They moved by themselves. The maestros looked at me admiringly. "Oh, that gal, what talent, what poise."

I didn't do more than my body asked of me. I just moved naturally, no more. With hands at rest, because those crazy women who get on stage and begin to gesticulate as if making faces, those wind-up dolls don't have anything to do with art.

Hands are made of flesh, not wood, and they belong to the body, controlled by the brain and the will.

A woman's hand has to be held in. Very close to her side and her waist, not in the air whirling about.

One hand moves, the other rests, and when you use both, either to sing or dance, you have to do so with great discretion.

Naughtiness is done with the hand, a side of the hand close up to the mouth. Sadness, with hands clasped and near the belly button. Cajoling, with both hands on the waist or one through the hair, like stroking it.

That's the game of hands, more or less, because the other details, the whole body, the voice, which has to be full, the diction, clear, well formed sentences, the eyebrows, the face, that goes along with the message, be it sad or happy.

To know and master those realms of dramatic art, maestros don't count.

Experience with the audience and well-intentioned criticism are indispensable. Criticism, not diatribes.

I left there unhappy, it's true. My heart was split in two with no spirit left. I was too young to have lost the love of my life.

Even today when I hear the word Tivoli a whole bunch of cockroaches come into my mind. Horrors!

Thinking it over carefully, I escaped from the devil. I look back and in spite of all the bad things, I laugh. I learned to take things lightly.

Little bells, little bells! I forget easily, I don't hold a grudge. I learned that from Cubans. We're forgetful. We get kicked, shoved, and the next day we're giving everybody parties. Whether that's good or bad, I don't know. Mama never forgot my father. She made her life into a carnival fair, but there was my father, for good or for ill.

Without even talking about him, I knew when she had him on her mind. In good restaurants, when we went for a boat ride, in good wine, my father was there. Mama never forgot him. And he was cruel, leaving her in a country that wasn't hers, with no papers, with no money, nothing. In the chifferobe I still keep a German watch chain that was my father's.

And I hear him. Ofelia, who knows me well, says they're voices I make myself hear. But I swear again and again that I don't. I hear clear as a bell, without narcotics or witchcraft. It's probably that he needs a mass . . . And it isn't a matter of sickliness either. If there's a healthy woman in the world, I'm it.

"You spend your life talking foofarah. What a silly you are!"

"Pardon me but everybody talks about their own affairs."

"Well keep it up, dummy, because they're going to shoot you out of here faster than a cannonball, for being an idiot, an idiot."

"Have them get me out of here, that's all, I've already done enough. And if there's no help for it, I'll go to Purgatory. What I want is for them to finish taking me away, goddamn it!"

But nothing. They didn't get me out. I left on my own two feet. I didn't tell Mama a thing. I decided and later Havana found out. I'm talking about the year '08. I had just turned twenty.

Without work, without a husband, without support from society.

I ran around the capital almost barefoot, and I'm not exaggerating. Good relations and clean dealings made me deserving of many people's confidence and affection. Thanks to that, in the middle of that cyclone, I continued to take dance classes. I wasn't going to leave the theater for anything in the world. That was all a three or four month *impasse*. I had my nest egg, some five hundred pesos, and with that I could navigate. Beaus came and went. And I gave them all the gate. My spirit had not revived much after the death of my husband.

Those who knew the story looked at me with a certain distrust. There was no one who could stop believing the boy committed suicide on my account. That's life. But me, soaring and ringing, with a great desire to rise high and show my mettle.

I didn't want to get into big companies, or the *zarzuela*. I was offered castles and kings, but I declined. I was patient. My big opportunity hadn't arrived. Those things all performers wait for, applause, lights, flowers, a suitor with spark were a thousand miles away from me in those years. But I remained placid in spite of my temperament.

I studied, I calmed down, I learned to gather my lines like a fisherman.

My house lit up all of a sudden. A downpour of gold came, I don't know where so much money came from. The thing is that Mama and I decided to go to Europe for a few months. And we went.

José Miguel Gómez of the Liberal Party had just announced his candidacy. A very tranquil and very accommodating man. He defeated Menocal who only cared for the high life. The typical business man. Owner of the

Chaparra sugar plantation and many other things. It was because of that that we all were happy with Gómez' victory.

A resounding and deserved victory.

We left the port of Havana in the month of February, 1909. It was the cold season and the boat set sail on a day when the temperature dropped like never before on this island. What a thrill! To set out on an adventure is the most exciting thing there is. We spent whole days and nights on that boat. Drinking, getting to know rich men, millionaires, playing poker, Spanish cards, roulette . . . the life of an Indian princess. I pinched myself to make sure it was real.

I mingled with the best of Havana. No one needed to know who I was or what I did. So I played the part of the grand dame, I enjoyed myself, took pleasure in the beauty. I was happy, after all. If I played a certain number, it came up. Thirteen or seven, which are my war horses.

If I put on a more or less revealing dress the whole boat wanted to get to know me. The truth is that the voyage pulled me out of the swamp.

I came to forget the grief and I survived.

One night it was announced that there was an officer in the crew who sang. He was daring enough to go out on the floor and do his little number. He sang worse than a street hawker. The orchestra wasn't at all bad, I kid you not. A band of trumpets, kettledrums, piano, it was alright. It had been months since I'd heard good rumba. And I asked the musicians if they could loosen up a bit.

They played a rumba, very badly, but I danced out on the floor. Alone, because no one dared to step out. It was an uproar. I had to stay in my cabin the rest of the voyage, playing solitaire and reading.

They knocked on my door, they hinted, they sent notes through Mama.

The captain made me a gift of a Veracruz silver bracelet with a heart-shaped onyx. I accepted it because he was the captain. Otherwise, I wouldn't have for anything in the world. One has to know how to value gifts. I accept them when they accompany admiration, not when they come full of lust. Then they're not gifts, but traps, hooks.

On a boat you read a lot. A young woman like myself, unaccustomed to reading, would get bored. I was horribly bored.

Nights on deck are lovely, but very cold. Every now and then I remembered Martí. They say that when he left Cuba he stood at the rail weeping. The day we set sail I went out and I too rested against the rail and saw Havana, El Morro, La Cabaña, Luz and Caballero Park, the whole city. I thought of José Martí and I felt like crying. It's hard to leave your country. Even though I knew I had to return. But it's hard, very hard.

We arrived in France and I cut my hair. I looked really good in a bob.

France is very beautiful. Enormous. The port of Le Havre is always full of fruits and fish. It all seems like theater props. Everyone there wore sideburns. Men of means and the common man. Handsome sideburns that ended at the jaw.

"All that you see there is Paris," my mother said.

It was the image of Paris. We got off the train with two suitcases and a leather bag full of sheet music, just in case.

The first thing I made out were the open air cafes, the tables.

Mama asked directions for the Bastille, but nobody could tell her. We got rooms in a hotel on Cujas Street. We lived there for the space of one week. The first two days I was terribly cold sleeping in a room with two beds. Then I left Mama by herself and I moved to the next room, with good heat and a double bed. That was all thanks to a little Italian named Pietro who worked at the reception desk. He was a great friend of Cuba, of our music.

We were waiting for the money my aunt was supposed to send from Vienna. Cujas Street is narrow and steep. Many bars and loads of Negroes.

Paris fascinated me. Two blocks from my hotel were the Luxembourg Gardens covered with snow, and down below at the end of the avenue, the Seine, broad and romantic. On the banks of the Seine was where I first ate roasted chestnuts.

"Merci, pardon, je vous adore," those were the phrases I learned in the seven days I enjoyed in Paris.

The money arrived and my mother went to buy a ticket to go by train from Paris to Vienna.

In the Latin Quarter, near Notre Dame, there's an Arab inn. The cheapest and the best in Paris. It's a little wooden house with a low roof. It faces the river. There I saw the girls from the Folies-Bergére. They went there to eat cous cous. The owner had a table reserved for them.

They arrived with handbags on their shoulders, very boisterous, and sat down.

They were quite beautiful. Very shapely with a style that was very authentic. The Folies was quite expensive and neither Mama nor I could go. Besides, in seven days you can't be at mass and in the procession too. The Seine, Notre Dame, the chestnuts, the snows of Luxembourg, that's the postcard I have kept from that trip to Paris. The City of Light. The Mecca of Art.

The important thing, I'd say, is that I was actually there, I saw it all and its charm stayed with me, the halo that appears above a saint's head. That's greater than remembering like some idiot the name of the streets, this church or that . . .

In less than eight days I saw more than some see in a year. Pietro was my guide and with him I saw all the important museums in Paris. Italians love museums and relics. That's why we went to the Louvre three times in a row. When we got out of there I almost couldn't walk because my feet had swollen up like balloons. Nonetheless, we go to a cafe to spend the evenings, near the Opera, where poets and musicians gathered. Since it was cold at night, the cafe's big windows were closed, and the smoke inside and the noise drove me crazy. They read their poems and their songs. And they sang as loud as their throats could stand. The Italian got a grass called "hashish" and smoked it like mad. He told me he felt he was on the high seas and he rowed and all . . . I never dared smoke it. What I did was smell it awhile and then I got happy too because otherwise I was bored to tears. My legs went soft and my head spun all around the hall. That grass, the foulest smelling stuff, they picked it like we do coffee. They laughed, cried with their eyes wide open, sang . . . it was great fun, but the next day you had to take acids to cure yourself. As you were leaving the place, smelling all that, the whole of Paris stank the same way. The odor got into your nose and no perfume could remove it. One day, as I'm leaving that cafe, it occurs to me to sing and I sang with a thin, sharp soprano voice, like I've never had. It was nothing more than the miracle that came from smelling that stuff. Pietro laughed like an idiot because the next night my voice wouldn't come out, not even when I tried. The night Mama and I caught the train for Vienna I had a few drinks with the Italian in the bar there in the Station. It was our farewell. Pietro stood next to our coach and from inside I could see him. I felt a strange thing, as if I were going to cry. I imagine on account of the drinks I'd had. What I do know is that I didn't see only him. There were lots of people behind him, and they looked like the ones from the cafe. Now, I never found out whether it was an optical illusion, whether I was drunk or if those people, in fact, were there. I never knew.

Paris stupefied me. And when we arrived in Vienna, everything seemed tiny, reduced to its smallest scale.

Vienna is a dreamy city, sad but dreamy. The Opera has the biggest chandelier in the world. Later I heard it said that Caruso made it sway with a high note. I don't believe it. That chandelier was exquisite.

My aunt treated us very well. She took us to the theater several times. She dressed us and gave us shoes. She was a rich woman, married to the owner of a well-known sweet shop in Austria.

In those days people thought about flying in balloons made of cloth.

I remember a gigantic park and some balloons going up with great fanfare, crowds of people, an orchestra and all that God would have commanded. It was the height of exhibitionism. Airplanes already existed but those clowns in colored balloons were still around. It was risky to go so high without a motor, no brakes or rudder. It gave me a chill! I would have given my life to fly for half an hour in one of those contraptions.

I saw that in Vienna when it was frighteningly cold.

My aunt's life was completely given over to the business. She inspected the sweet shop every afternoon. The girls who worked there came to dislike her. When I arrived, one of them asked me if I was going to live there. My mother understood and said no, we were just passing through, that we lived in Cuba.

The girl smiled as if feeling great relief for me. I think if I'd stayed there to work I would have become slave number one for my aunt. The Hungarians are Gypsies by nature.

They like to be globe trotters. Mama in Cuba. My aunt in Austria. And other aunts and uncles sprinkled all over the world.

That trip was delirious. I remember the countryside of Austria, white with streaks of green. The little houses with tiled roofs, poppies and pots in the windows.

Austria is cold. The freezing air gets in your pores, and your ears and nose hurt just by touching them.

I hate a cold climate. It makes me feel useless, stiff and shaky. Mama withstood it better than me because of her origins. I never asked her why the devil it occurred to her to make the trip in the middle of winter. For me it was the test of champions. Austria, Vienna rather, is a place for the good life. There you didn't see poverty, beggars, peddlers . . . I kid you not! That was a paradise of luxuries. The people lived well regardless of the seasonal restrictions. They all wore suits. And the women, plush hats. Church was very crowded. Sundays were a time to be withdrawn, to walk in the park, go to church and spend the day resting next to the stove. Then the war came and all that ended, they say.

I marvelled at Austria. It's the dreamy country par excellence, lover of good music and art.

That's where *The Merry Widow* premiered.

They say God gives a beard to him who has no chin, and it's true.

She herself, old and all, wrinkled and all, dressed like a first lady. It was fame, not prestige but fame.

I would say she was obligated to go through all those maneuvers. For her, to enter the Encanto dressed in one color and leave in another was all the same thing.

She liked the Encanto for the French perfumes and the hats.

A bit short and plump, with those broad brimmed Italian straw hats edged in lilac and lemon yellow. What a woman . . !

They say, but don't believe me, that she was a devoted daughter. But she didn't take her mother around much, at least I never met her.

Rachel in the Encanto was a spectacle. When she came in the Galiano Street door, the main entrance, it seemed as if a circus had come in.

The young men stood with mouths open, because she enticed without cunning, as performers can do.

Lovers and degenerates are a whole other story. I don't know anything about that.

I can't say. I was an employee there and nothing more. "Oh, dearie, find me a shade that suits me," she paid whatever it cost and left waving: "Goodbye, girls."

She's probably already dead, or close to it, from old age.

Unless she's been preserved in a bottle of formaldehyde.

I've never been a woman of habit, I mean, methodical. I've been crazy about tours, globe trotting, seeing beautiful places, meeting different people . . . But as months passed and that cold and that language which I just couldn't learn, and my mother neurasthenic, I began to want to go back. My aunt often went out with her husband and we'd stay in the house listening to music because we were indisposed by the cold.

One night, now that it comes to mind, Mama prepared a good hot tea for when my aunt returned. She set a pretty table, with those cloth place mats and those little silver spoons. My aunt came in and sat down with her husband to have tea. We waited for him to go up to bed. We didn't know how to tell my aunt that we were dying to return to Cuba. She and Mama talked in their language for a long while. I was so nervous that I forgot to drink the tea, already ice cold. My aunt arranged my scarf and touched my nose with her cold little fingers. She said to me in a chop suey Spanish: "Cold, my girl, very cold." It seems my aunt understood everything exactly because Mama looked at me and said : "I'm asking your aunt to buy us a return ticket tomorrow."

I don't know why so many things crowded into my mind. I saw Havana so clearly, the streets, the theaters, the beaches. How happy I was knowing we were going to return! I left all those people without any sadness at all. They came to say goodbye and I didn't cry or anything. I sat quite comfortably in the train that was taking us to the port, and saw my aunt, her husband and the girls from the sweet shop with their hankies, and I, as if it had nothing to do with me. I began to eat candy so the time would go faster. Later I was sorry I behaved that way with relatives. But . . . What can you do? My goal was to get here, to my country, even though what was waiting for me was still hell. The voyage on the ship lasted a century. A century!

Chapter Two

Two big events took place on my return to Cuba. People were horrified with the appearance of Halley's comet. And the death of one of the most popular men in Havana. Yarini.

About Halley's comet you can go on forever. It arrived unexpectedly. All Havana was moved. People cried from fright. There were people who died of heart attacks, of choking. We weren't prepared. A people accustomed to conductor Roig's open air concerts, the rocking chair, the park, idle talk . . . We weren't made for that kind of bustle. But the it appeared with its luminous horse's tail and left everybody astounded. Pharmacies couldn't supply enough smelling salts. Enormous lines every morning to buy sedatives. Nobody could figure it out. The comet there, standing still, behind the Marola del Morro, threatening to slash out with his tail.

And the little girls in their attics with telescopes to see it up close. In my house there was no telescope, and we had to rent one for 10 centavos to be able to enjoy the spectacle.

Many pregnant women saw the comet pass by and gave birth to strange children, with red marks, some with a tail and all, on their rump and back. People said that the comet itself had been reflected there. Who knows!

"Looks like taffy, looks like a yellow boa, it's a fire snake," said América, a little colored girl who lived in the slums.

I've always been very level-headed. I haven't been a coward. But since I didn't know a shred of astronomy, I was a bit scared. The comet impressed the Holy Mother. Gutiérrez Lanza himself, an expert on stars, was silent for several entire days, without daring to put his eye to the telescope. They say it's because he was afraid of facing up to the truth.

Halley threatened to touch the earth. On the 18th of May, the appointed day, people gathered with their families, girlfriends and boyfriends, mothers and children, but nothing. It didn't touch anything. It went away without a peep. In 1985 it will appear again. I don't think I'll be able to see it. But if I make it, I'll look for a good telescope because the way things are, the advances in science, in astronomy itself, you don't have to be afraid of any star.

Much less that one, since you already know it won't do any damage.

There's Halley, fixed like an eye, suspended in the air in the mornings, looking everywhere like an inspector of the infinite.

Fetus of the world, bullfighter with no pigtail.

The voice of the inhabitants of Halley's sphere has got to be seventy-five times louder than the voice of our people: it would seem to us that there, if we could hear it, they talk with artillery in their mouths. As we look up at the sky, death captures us, wraps us in the enormous whirlwind of universal life, and as atoms and dust, we are incorporated into the cosmos without ever knowing either what we are nor from whence we came, nor where we are going, nor why we live nor why we die, or what any of this is or all of this which surrounds us, poor blind men whose eyes can not see.

La Discusión, 1 May, 1910

We become accustomed to everything, we tire of all splendors and we become habituated to the most extraordinary events; the most brilliant stars, the most beautiful planets still enchant us, but they no longer surprise us.

They belong to a sky that lights up every night, the North Star is nothing but a hanging lantern, the morning star only an accessory for the songs of mandolins, the Big Dipper and Little Dipper merely pretexts for the nocturnal erudition of life in summer castles . . .

Where from, where to?
Who without quarter condemns you to travel on?
What mission is destined for your luminous shining?
Will you perhaps crash into our grain of sand?
La Discusión, 9 May, 1910

Yarini was a horse of a different color. His death moved the whole population because he was a refined young man, elegant, from a good family. Not a savage.

I've heard many comments about him. Conceited people who talk just to talk. A young person's life in those years wasn't like it is today. There was different way of doing things. Today what you call a pimp is a sad imbecile, with no place to hang his hat, with no authority. The pimp from Madrid is something else, again. The pimp from Lavapiés. Well, that was more or less how our pimps were in the years 1910 or 1915. The word pimp is pejorative, very ugly.

I'd say the pimps from Havana weren't fond of making trouble. They got along with the ladies, the decent ones and the loose ones too, but they did it all with civility. Cuban pimps have been kind, very generous and accommodating.

A French pimp is very different. Vain, bullying, mean, quarrelsome, exploitative . . .

All of the talk going around today about Yarini is half true and half invented by the common people. To become famous in an environment like the one in this country is very simple. Any Joe Blow one day and the next, boom!

Now Yarini is like a saint or a hero. Some famous thing. That's due to the lack of real news because he never went beyond being a pimp. The pimp from the barrio of San Isidro. Women who make a living from their sex, prostitutes, to speak clearly, fall in love. They're women of flesh and blood just like the others, but a little looser, with no pretense.

Yarini had his harem. Women just crazy about him. They drooled, they spread their legs. I can understand that illusion. For me to love an arrogant man is the greatest thing there is. Nobody falls in love with a hypocrite. But with a tyrant like him, I can believe it. I myself, without ever having spoken to him, just having seen him walking around, was sort of fascinated. He was something impossible. The type of male who didn't give himself easily. You had to beg him, tell him stories, give him winks. What an age! Today you don't see that. Today love is a vulgarity. Sign a paper, have a pack of kids, like little rabbits, a mother-in-law . . . Horrors! Before things weren't like that, so cold. There was mystery, secrecy in relationships. To be able to say I live with Alberto Yarini was very difficult for any woman, for anyone.

You start to hear people say the silliest things and it makes you laugh. Right now, here in the city of Havana, the ones who didn't know how Yarini behaved say that what he liked to do was slice women's tits with a pocket knife and when he fought with a man, to knife him in the butt. All of that is a product of Cuban imagination.

He was exquisite.

"Miss, be so kind. Young man, please."

That was Yarini, Alberto Yarini.

That's why they killed him cold, like a pig.

It's sad for a man to die like that, so full of life.

Even more so a beautiful man. So he had his underhanded dealings. Who doesn't? So he was mixed up in the white slave trade, alright, who around here hasn't gotten away with murder? Poor man, to think that the worms ate him up

. . . with his spotless white clothes, his watch chain, his straw hat . . . Poor man.

The morgue in Havana was swarming. People were standing at the railings, peering in at the windows, coming in the doors . . . Yarini was the object of wide spread sympathy among the people.

All the whores from Havana crowded around to see the body brought out. Not even the King of Spain had a bigger crowd. They brought piles of flowers. He died at 27, a good age for a man to triumph. I was a faithful friend of Yarini's. I was there until the last moment. I put his tie on him, I shaved him, combed him, closed his eyes. A dead man who has been like a brother doesn't make you feel disgust. He was, without exaggeration, the most sought after souteneur in Cuba. His loyalty, his polish, carried him to that level. As far as I know, she never saw him or dealt with him.

The women we had were common. Rachel wasn't. Rachel was showy, an artist, in short, of another cut.

In any case, she can speak about those years because she's as old as walking. But about Yarini, about his intimate life, no one knows him better than yours truly.

The day he died, the day of the skirmish, it was raining bucketfuls. And it was cold. A cold typical of Havana, with lots of wind and gusts. We were near that plaza called Caballerías, a wharf.

We'd gone to have drinks with two whores. The whores didn't suspect what was about to happen because they were novices. Just arrived, so to speak, country bumpkins, with the mountain smell still in their arm pits. But pretty; round, well made, with nice big asses.

Yarini gives me a wrist watch and tells me:

"Pinky, you shut your mouth."

In fact, whatever might come up, any business whatsoever, I arranged with him, and with no one else. But it seems that the climate had already heated up. And they'd already been around checking on him.

The French are a bad breed, among the worst.

And Yarini dared nothing less than pluck a pearl from their string.

Petite Bertha, the prettiest woman in San Isidro, Lolot's property, came to work for him. Lolot, who was evil, wouldn't put up with sweets being snatched from him and went after Yarini, to kill him, that very day, on that corner.

Life's coincidences. It was my lot to be present through it all. I even saw the bullet that did him in.

It's been almost 60 years since then and a shiver still runs down my legs when I think about that shootout.

I'll let my head be cut off if there weren't more than three of them shooting at him. High on top of the houses on San Isidro street, on the houses or on the balconies, but more than three of them, because it sounded like a war.

Those revolvers weren't quiet like the ones today. The shot that killed him went through his cheekbone, the right one. Yarini reared up when he felt the bullet. "Balls, Pinky," he said to me. The whores took off running and I got behind a wall because I was unarmed. I didn't see him fire, but I know he did, because they found him with a little .38 in his hand. The only shot he managed to get off hit the Frenchie from Marseille, one-eyed and freckled, and messed him all up.

I up and fled, the whores did the same. Later I showed up at the morgue to take care of him. I arrived crying. A friend is a friend, especially when there have been trials and tribulations.

He was purple, his face was a block of ice, purple and skinny. Death is monstrous! It made me feel sorry, not disgusted. His family didn't touch him. It was a well-to-do family, father a dentist, mother at home.

A family from Havana, from Galiano.

They sent a coffin to put Yarini in. It was the only thing they did. He turned out to be the black sheep of the family and that can't be forgiven.

Petite Bertha went to the burial, she risked her life to lead the procession.

They say she had fallen in love with him, which is possible, but I don't believe it. She went to make the French jealous and so they could see she didn't fear anything.

Everybody who was anybody in those days was at Yarini's funeral. Even the nation's President, señor José Miguel Gómez.

The cortege left from Havana. People on foot following the wreaths. The balconies full. It seemed like a day of national mourning. I was stunned because when it has to do with a brother of yours, it hurts more.

As we arrived at Calzada de Zapata the French souteneurs began to pick fights. They formed into groups, with knives in their pockets. They wanted to avenge the Marseillaise's death by killing one of us. I would have been a perfect target for them.

The police cordoned off the area, but to no avail. Anyway the row was violent. I hid behind the hearse and thanks to that I'm still alive and here to tell about it. But Petite Bertha was wounded in a breast.

So, bleeding, she got to the cemetery. That's what you call a woman.

The wreaths were blown up, into smithereens. People scattered through the dirt streets of Vedado, but after half an hour the mob was organized again. The man had to be buried amidst shots and knife thrusts. With God's help, it was done.

The newspapers reported the events as newspapers always do, whatever seems right to them.

You could say that that death was truly felt. Later came Chibás, Rita Montaner, Benny Moré, who also had very crowded funerals. But none were like Yarini's. Let Bertha say it wasn't so, she still lives on Condesa Street, older than La Cabaña, but well preserved.

Bertha for short. They never could pronounce my last name here. It's long and difficult: Chateaubriand. But I just have them call me Bertha.

What I want is to die. Let them come to take me away. I can't endure a life like this one. It's a dog's life. I just want to die.

I lost my memory for details. I don't have any strength. I can't even get up from this armchair. I'm full of veins. I'm just waste.

The only thing I can say is he left a 20 franc coin, a Spanish gold coin, and 5 pesos. It was all he had in his pockets. I don't know any more. I don't even want to remember. I'm innocent.

Besides, you should leave the poor boy in peace, he has enough to grieve for, let him rest.

This city traps you. A Cuban woman seems to walk on air, not on the pavement. A Cuban man the same. We are gifted with a fleeting happiness. We don't expect a death or an accident either. That's why people are so emotional and cry and shout and stamp their feet if something happens that isn't part of the daily routine.

The people in this country amaze me. They are what has come to be known as a happy people, who live in a paradise and forget hell is the other part. People like that are admirable. Few of us have that gift. We all carry around a type of vain optimism. The birdie singing in the storm. The worst things here are fixed up with drums and beers.

Yesterday and today. That is a destiny. A grand destiny because if not, my poor people would be wasted, faithless.

I became enthusiastic again encountering this flowering place, the rowdy streets, the crowded parks, music halls, the barrio atmosphere itself, and since things had gotten ugly for my old lady, I began to look for work.

Also because what was running through my veins was music, like with Schubert.

A person addicted to rhythm, with a good ear, a figure and a desire to please, had already won half the battle. I fought like a fiend. I hit the street. I wouldn't go back to that place in Palatino, not even for a treasure. I aspired to acting. Dancing, singing a little and above all, acting. I found a little friend who went with me to theaters at night. We'd make the rounds all over Havana: the Moulin Rouge, the Albizu, the Comedia, all of them. My little friend, so he could go out with me, bought my tickets and meals. Afterward we would sit in the Prado to share our business. I was mostly silent, he was the one who had a head full of weird ideas, but he was knowledgeable and I was in the dutiful position of listening. Not a single detail escaped me. In a few matters I even dared to give him advice.

The poor guy was having a love affair that wasn't working out. One of those affairs that's not a true romance or a pastime either, because one side worships and the other gets worshipped. Well, my friend was very naive. He fell in love at first sight, without taking into account the quality of the individual, his origin, his behavior. I told him to think things through but it was like talking to the wall. Every day was tears and comedy. Unhappy creature. That kind of angel still exists.

Adolfo did my makeup, he taught me to bring out my eyebrows, to comb myself, to speak English . . . I came to feel affection for him and he for me, truth be told. Thanks to that friendship I met many dancers, chorus girls, impresarios. I never dared go into a theater alone.

Adolfo gave me something every month. Handkerchiefs, lipsticks, stockings. He was the one who made me see how much a woman, how attractive I was.

"Take a good look at yourself, you're wasting your time, silly."

But he had a flaw, he was terribly jealous. The man who approached me was the man he found fault with. One day we went to a small costume party He dressed as a Dutch girl, he looked really cute, and I as a noble Andalusian.

41

We had the best costumes of the night. The place was in an uproar. I learned a few phrases and the Andalusian came out just right. Later in the Alhambra I did the Andalusian many times, remembering that party. Adolfo himself took me by the hand to the studio of El Sevillano, a great dance teacher in Havana.

It was there that I studied systematically for the first time, hours on end, holding on to the bar, lifting my leg. I'd leave a little puddle of sweat on the floor the size of a fry pan when I was done.

El Sevillano had no hope for me, as a chorus girl I mean. He told me I was a natural rumbera. But not a ballerina. I paid no attention. I answered:

"Stick to teaching me technique, I'll do the rest myself."

That, I believe, was the proper answer for a star. Sometimes teachers don't see their student's talent and they mislead them. That's why I got along so well with Adolfo because he always said to me:

"Rachel, you're an actress. Don't you do anything but that."

Adolfo saw only one side of me. He wanted me to be a tragic figure, or a character actress. I always let him have his way. I didn't want to disappoint him, but what I had inside wasn't that. Even though he knew me well, he was mistaken about that. I was not only a, how to say it, budding actress, but a social barometer, what my country remembers me for.

As far as I'm concerned she's a woman without age. And with a lot of youth inside.

Jovial, a jovial lady.

She gets telephone calls everyday from young men and some slightly older ones.

She spends hours and hours stuck to the phone. I don't know what they say to her, especially the one who calls at four, but she flirts with him and laughs at him.

She won't let him come to the house because her present husband is very jealous. 80 years old and jealous. If that's what you can call jealousy because I'd say it was more like a sickness. Men whose cerebral cortex has gotten weak on them and they don't progress.

One time I asked her:

"Ma'am, tell me if you would, how old are you?"

"As old as your mother when she had you, you fresh thing."

I didn't expect that answer, because the lady, with her life and all, is a very courteous woman.

Chapter Three

Adolfo knew all the tactics and the inner workings of the theater world.

The poor thing, he never got anywhere, his aspirations were shattered.

He worked in a cafe when what he dreamed about was being a dancer. But fate is like that. He did everything for me or on my behalf. Since he couldn't make it, I was going to with his help.

He contributed everything he could find. But always aimed at making me into a character actress.

We rehearsed together, improvising a stairway with a forest behind it and marble benches that we made with fish crates. Adolfo entered wearing a white tunic and called for me. Then I, crouching behind a push-broom column, answered like a jealous kitty.

"Here I am, dear."

That was the beginning of the first act of the vaudeville piece *Mark Antony and Cleopatra*. I, of course, was Cleopatra.

We didn't try to find an audience because we were beginners and Adolfo, deep down, was afraid he'd be razzed.

Those intimate moments of emotional release helped me to develop as an actress and to memorize long scripts. Memory, the betrayer . . !

Our repertoire was a whole string of sketches, classical works like *Hamlet*, vaudeville skits, two zarzuelas.

Afterward, we'd be worn out and we'd go for days without seeing each other. The classes at 63 Concordia Street continued.

"Lift your legs, your arms, lower your shoulders, hold up your chin."

I thought I was going to go crazy with so much up and down.

After a few months I danced flamenco with the best, rumba like the most genuine colored woman, and the habanera and polka, and even the softer rhythms: waltzes, fox trots, ballads.

Adolfín called me up for an accounting. We went to the small Lover's Park and he gave me an address.

"Take this and go without fail."

I took his advice and went. He refused to go with me so they wouldn't think that I went around with his kind, because the boy had his "little air of independence" and that doesn't look good.

I arrived at the home of a decent man who made me comfortable in the living room and the first thing he said to me was: "Miss, I've heard about you. I know that you do everything, that you move well and are accomplished, but the only thing that displeases me is that you come recommended by a creature who adds nothing of benefit to your person."

He was referring to Adolfo, naturally. A light went on in my head and I replied:

"Look here, Sir, I'm a girl who knows how to distinguish between the good, the so-so, and the bad. Adolfo is an acquaintance of mine with whom I do not have, as you might suppose, any intimacy whatever. He has spoken very highly of you to me and of the circus and I hope that we can understand each other without entering into details of a personal nature."

"No, What I wanted to say was . . ."

And I stunned him. These impresarios who think they can make you into a sap, what they need is a forceful answer like that. Alright, within a month, the man had me in the first balcony. With my cunning and natural grace, I had him in my pocket. I made him spend all the money he had on a new tent. He bought it and he gave the circus the name I had suggested to him: The Marvels of Austria, in memory of that country I love so much.

But the common people called it the Marvels circus, for short, and so we went around the country with that name, from the cape of San Antonio to the point of Maisí, in wagons, in automobiles, in trains . . .

I preferred that to having to return to the Tivoli with its plague of horny old goats and its clamor. Mama didn't accompany me on the tour because she had to continue with her business. But she sent me a postcard with a little white doggie and the finest chain with a Virgin of Santa Lucía so I could guard against the evil eye.

I wrote her two or three times, and sent kisses to Adolfo. The owner wouldn't let me receive sealed correspondence, but I always gave new addresses because each town I entered was already my territory. Wherever, I had a house, friends. If in Coliseo, then Coliseo, if in Tunas, then Tunas. I brought the character of the mulatta to the national scene. All the other girls were envious of the applause for me. And I said to myself: "For each hypocritical statement, a kiss on the cheek." With that policy I went strutting around in that little circus, amidst those human beasts.

The owner was about sixty badly-lived years old. He had always been in troupes of buffoons, in circuses, with burlesque groups, comedians, chorus girls. He was irresponsible. What you call a scoundrel.

He liked me from the day that I visited him at his house. But dummy that I am, I didn't realize that and lost a lot of time worrying, not because I was in love with him, but because his love for me could open all doors immediately, at least in that little circus. And that's how it was. To say

Rachel was to say Don Anselmo's spoiled little girl. I used all my little tricks to work less than anyone and stand out more. I pretended I was hoarse so I didn't have to stretch for songs in a high pitched key. Used swelling in my hands as an excuse not to carry things or move them around on the set. Everything was done for me, or nothing. I lived up to what I learned from my mother and from Adolfo, to always find my place. I faked pregnancy when I didn't want to dance the final rumba which is the most tiring thing there is. I faked a stiff neck so I didn't have to do the fawning mulatta. Then, that afternoon I'd go out straight as a stake, say two or three jokes and leave the same way. I faked being distressed so the owner would bring me vanilla ice cream. Faking is very simple. You can't imagine how simple it is. Much less recognize it. Just imagine the results and you'll see that without some of these tricks, the greatest entertainer would go under.

The impresarios, when they know how to be impresarios, have this business of pretending. If they don't, the performers will leave, disenchanted. Don Anselmo was very tolerant with everyone in the circus, not only with yours truly, in that regard.

Because of that, I lasted there some two years, doing acrobatics, dancing, singing traditional tunes, guarachas, ballads, parading like a vamp, like a prude, like a homebody. To parade around, that is to say, do nothing more than show myself on stage in order to fill the place up. I blew up balloons, romped about with rubber balls, swung in a flying trapeze, which gave me terrible shivers. I swallowed . . . no, I never got to sword swallowing, I couldn't. There was a Peruvian woman of about 40 who could do it marvelously, with swords and fire.

I was the silly clown and the evil one, the rogue.

I had a ball. It was my first experimental job. The first thing that was my own.

The Marvels of Austria had its difficulties. And me with it. But over and above the upheaval there was adventure and lust. We were all young in that troupe. The only grey haired one was Don Anselmo. He suffered a lot on account of that.

The first tour we made started from the train station, with a solid contract to perform in Esperanza, Santa Clara, Cienfuegos and other little towns in the province of Las Villas. We seemed like a Gypsy band, clean and moral, of course. We boarded the little train. Some of us were acquainted already, others weren't. But a tour leads to a profound knowledge of people. You see them at all hours of the day and in all sorts of duties. At waking up time, with sand in their eyes, at lunch time, at siesta, at dinner, in the toilet, at the time for sex.

It's terrible to live among human beings. Things fall apart because people don't have any control.

Don Anselmo fell madly in love with me. It was painful to see him at my feet, drooling. He'd bring me water: "A little sip, my love." At all hours.

He wouldn't let anyone come in my cubbyhole, because that wasn't a dressing room or even a turkey's head. Oh, God! that grouchy, dirty old man—who could have told me, that I, so young, would have to joust with cadavers. But that's how it was, just how it was. I like him deep down, let's cut the hypocrisy . . . The difference in age is a stimulant for love. You're the loved one and the old guy pays and puts up with it, and if he doesn't put up with it, he gets the boot and that's that. Because of my womanly pride, I love that. But it bothers me at the same time. Above all at the high point, the moment to be passionate. A young man is not the same as an old one. The advantage of the older man is that he demands nothing and the younger one, if he's a bumblebee, will leave you all dried up. Don Anselmo went to bed with me several times, in my moments of weakness. And it cost him dearly.

The circus was coming out ahead because I was enthusiastic and pulled out all my artistic stops. I arranged the programs, with me always at the center, I hired a pair of buffoons, a trio, two more clowns, I brought in a rubber woman, a "ventriloquack," a baritone and two girls who did the

48

finale with me when we gave a special performance. The colors of the new tent attracted customers. And in those country towns, so dead, having no other entertainment—the people would come out in droves and pack the stands. Loads of people came early with sandwiches and bottles of water, bought their tickets and sat in the stands to wait, asleep. It was in Santa Clara where the program came together best. It's a city with a lot of coming and going: street vendors, businesses, other troupes.

Everything passes through there. It's a town full of dust, dirt, but with a great deal of activity.

We set up the circus on the outskirts, at the end of San Cristóbal street, near the Market. The roustabouts were agile, good kids almost all.

When we arrived it occurred to me to buy a "Cuban" dress I had seen in a shop window. I dressed up in a Cuban flag, the star in the middle of my chest and the blue borders draped over my arms. The typical national costume. We went in a caravan announcing: There goes the Cubana!

THE MARVELS OF AUSTRIA
MANY ACTS
FUN AND LAUGHTER WITH THE
SPECIAL APPEARANCE OF
RACHEL
And
Others
Clowns-Comedians
Trios-Buffoons-Baritones
Swordswallowers
Tickets 10 centavos
Today in Santa Clara

And me as the banner carrier, parading about with the white end in my right hand.

That's how a performance should be announced. Santa Clara took a liking to me. I was the only leading actress who strolled alone through the park at an hour when seeing a woman on the street was quite rare.

Parks in the interior are divided by an invisible stripe, whites to one side, the preferred one of course, and coloreds to the other. It's always been that way in Santa Clara. A great deal of racism. Few coloreds went to the circus. And those who went perched way up, at the top of the stands. That's the way it should be.

Off season was the dead period. The sugar cane crop is what decides everything. Cane is the queen of Cuba. She's the one who orders and commands. When it's the off season a bumpkin doesn't have anything in his pockets.

The slack period in the circus. Few came and the few who did were almost always gate crashers, children in abundance, rickety bumpkins. An audience that doesn't inspire enthusiasm. They came to see the clowns and the acrobats.

Me, the most I did was sing a bit, talk with the performers . . . I began to feel suffocated. Who's going to do a rumba for an audience full of children!

The island of Cuba becomes sad in the off season. Nobody does anything.

The countryside wears mourning clothes.

And since people get to thinking, out come the tricks, bad tempered pranks.

I was brought down by fanaticism. The fanaticism of my fellow men and women in the circus. The fanaticism of hate. One day the tent was burned on one side and the wife of the night watchman accused me of being the instigator.

It's one of those stories of the vicissitudes of a decent artist in an atmosphere of envy.

No one was ignorant of my relationship with the old man, my fights, my disdain. And when that thing burned, they said "She did it, it can't be anyone else. She did it on purpose, to screw us, so we'd be out on the street." The whole Gypsy tribe fell on me. The Gypsy curse. The only one who didn't believe the slander was that unfortunate Don Anselmo. He called us together to make a report, and we each gave our own version.

Me, as soon as I saw how bad my standing was on account of the envy and the hatred, I started to cry. Don Anselmo stopped the meeting and calmed me down.

"Look here kid, if you did it, tell me why."

Nope, so he suspected me like the others. But I say unless they catch you with your hand in the cookie jar, you're innocent.

The tent was streaked with black but it wasn't ruined.

Later there were two or three more little blazes and nobody said a peep. In the end, the old man covered it all up so he could tickle me, because that's how old folks are.

But the 72 hours I was in the Esperanza police station nobody can take that away from me because, en masse, they accused me.

The first night I spent quietly. I ate a bunch and smoked a cigarette.

I woke up the next day with a terrible headache. I complained and they brought me a package of pills. The guard was divine.

He told me I was very serious, that I didn't talk. So I asked him:

"Tell me, you, what month were you born in?

"Me, in January."

"Then, we have the same sign, Aquarius, the two of us. See, now my fear's gone away for sure. I can stay here a year. I'm not afraid of a thing."

I had him in my pocket. Later he recommended that I not speak or get nervous the day of the trial they were going to have. And if I had set fire to the tent, not to ever confess it.

The bitches said I had fixed up a strip of burlap tied to a plate and given it to a colored boy, that they had seen me, that besides the burlap the colored boy had gotten money and

51

that I was disloyal and a bandit. The one who suffered most was Don Anselmo seeing me stuck in that tug o'war. The night watchman's wife was thrown out of the circus with her husband and all. I stayed on because I was the soul of the circus. Those are the things that happen when people want to cause harm. What consoles me is that the law of the fittest always works.

I don't say that with a strip of burlap . . .

Does she lie, she does. But they're white lies. Sometimes with a little poison, but little lies after all is said and done.

We kept on touring. Our troupe was like a balloon. It would get inflated and then deflated again . . . because many guys and dolls got hooked up together in the middle of the tour, they'd abandon everything or go to another circus, or they'd take to living in Tunas or Cienfuegos. That's show people, adventuresome, giddy, raucous . . .

Every time one would leave, there'd be 10 or 15 candidates who'd arrive with their little suitcases, and their rags, to offer themselves. They could just as soon swallow fire as play the sax as lie down on a bed of nails.

It was the need for food. In those years there was hunger in Cuba. And many political whirlwinds.

The old man convinced me to stay: "I'll put up with anything you do, kid, do whatever you want, kill me if you wish, but you're my life."

Hearing that daily I softened up out of pity and kept going with Don Anselmo on my back.

Whatever kind of compromising position he'd catch me in, the most he'd do would be to advise me not to waste my time, etc, etc.

Poor Don Anselmo! There are many sad, hopeless, life-sized puppets like him out there.

Women are fundamentally bad. We abuse men. I confess.

I spent my life telling her, "You, put a helmet on your head, doll, cover up your head, because one of these heavenly days that tent will fall on us, it's so old and rotten. It's going to squash us like cockroaches. Cover your head."

She, since they were all alike, are alike, laughed at me and looked me up and down, as if saying: "Look here, what I want from you . . ." and she's laughing so much I can grab her. That was during the trip to Santiago and I yanked her so hard I nearly pulled her arm off. What a gal! Too bad we were never able to get out of there. The old guy watched her with binoculars. Even so, we rolled around in the tent, in the sawdust . . . We would get under the stage and then come out all mussed up but happy. The old man, I think he knew but he didn't say anything. What a gal!

It all began and ended there, exactly like our act.

The conflagration caught us in Santiago de Cuba. They arrived there to impose order and frighten the citizens. They were animals with human masks.

Cuba didn't deserve that war, but it had it and it was between brothers. Negroes against whites.

They made chittlins of our circus, they humiliated us, they threatened us with death by machete, especially Don Anselmo, if we didn't give them food.

We gave them everything, even the performers' costumes: muslins, piqués, taffetas . . .

That was the Negroes' little war, the racist rumpus of 1912. Because of that I don't think the Negro can be given much freedom. They were going to impose themselves here if it hadn't been for the government's good sense.

Negroes are dangerous with a machete in their hands, very dangerous. The business, as I remember it, began with the thing about the Morúa Law. Morúa was a decent government man, but he had the misfortune of being mulatto.

He wanted to be famous and proposed a law prohibiting colored societies. Being a Negro, he shouldn't have done that. That law made him the enemy of many of his race and the matter reached all the way out to the bush.

Negroes rose up in the whole of Oriente province, in Las Villas, and I don't know if in Havana. Those were days of anxiety and stormy weather. Bolts, doors and windows all hermetically sealed in the towns and cities.

The panic spread because seeing that they were supported by the entire criminal element, the Negroes soared: "Haiti, this is probably another Haiti!"

The leaders Estenoz and Ivonet were classy Negroes. That's why they had followers. They fooled most everybody, promising them the world.

A patent leather republic was to be established here. The racists took advantage of the hills of Oriente province and climbed up with rifles, torches, generals' and brigadiers' uniforms...

We hid in the Villalba's house until the disturbance subsided. The entire troupe disbanded, some for Havana and others for who knows where.

The old man trembled because he had never seen a war between coloreds and whites. I would make him chamomile tea and calm him so he wouldn't up and die on me in the midst of that whirlwind. What would I do alone in Santiago de Cuba without money, without supporters?

The Negro population in the capital of the province hid. You'd go out on the street and not see a Negro for three miles around. They were intimidated, too. The town councils and the colored societies closed up.

Not a drum, not a party, nothing. And for them that was pure hell. The uprisings in Alto Songo and La Maya were the biggest. They say that Estenoz showed off with an American rifle and that Ivonet was like General Moncada. That's what the Santiagans said. Hearing that, I died inside. The poor people, they had to flee to little towns in flocks, to seek refuge in barracks or in the homes of relatives. Those were pilgrimages with no food, clothes or weapons.

They left their furniture in pawn shops and fled. Estenoz' troops invaded many little burgs and so did Ivonet's.

Except that Ivonet didn't have the caliber of a general and the other did, because he was a conceited, hawk nosed mulatto.

That war was carried out with a lot of rum. The leaders were drunks and vicious types. The best proof was given by General Monteagudo whose picture appeared in the press with two rebellious Negroes and several bottles of rum. Monteagudo was sent by President Gómez to clean up the area. Of course it took a lot of work but he succeeded. Mendieta is another of the officers who participated and who the whole country remembers gratefully. They knew that, with rum, the Negroes would be defeated. And from what I heard, the bottles climbed up the slopes so that the drunken Negroes would give up. Alcohol can do marvels.

They burned sugar mills and whole plantations but they couldn't win. They were in the minority and wrong besides. There was a lot of destruction in La Maya. The racists burned 800 houses, a town in flames. The train station, the inn and the post office.

La Maya was left in ashes! Later a song came out that went "Alto Songo burns La Maya" and I don't know what else. That's my country: after the war, a little bit of music.

Negroes, Negroes! What a headache they caused, my Lord.

The worst part of that stupid uproar was what they did to our flag. They took the shining star off the flag that had appeared in dreams to Narciso López and, in its place, they painted a colt as black as coal. Right there you can sum up the war: the colt against the star.

Whites got mixed up in it out of curiosity and it cost them dearly. A group of disloyal islanders formed up with the troops of the two little generals, Estenoz and Ivonet, and they were all liquidated. More than one islander was dragged on palm fronds to the cemetery, to the pigsty, to the cess pool . . .

The government's rage was so great that it has to be admitted that some indiscretions occurred. For instance, I remember in Santiago, it's said the same thing happened in Regla, that each time a white saw a Negro on the street he would shoot him. And so, many fell who most likely didn't even know who Estenoz or Ivonet were. Wars are like that. The just always pay for the sinners.

In Havana the fellows from Acera del Louvre flooded out into the streets, along Prado, down Zulueta, to the Malecón. Any Negro they saw who was sort of "prettied up," they cut his tie off. Now, to speak the truth, they were to blame. They threatened that this island would be colored territory, that Estenoz would be President and other monstrosities, that's why the white fellows revolted.

Under the custard apple tree in Prado, there was an old aristocrat, very refined, who had been one of the rebels. He told me the story of how the colored boys would sneak away each time they saw him. They'd lower their heads or cross the street. He stopped them good.

The agitation stirred up the whole island. There was no talk but of the racist racket. But since everything is the way it is, and no evil lasts 100 years, the situation calmed down when the Americans arrived. The Americans certainly were respected. They anchored a ship in the bay and the storm ended. They also announced that something like 500 lassoing cowboys would arrive, experts in roping wild steers.

If they came, it didn't say so in the papers, but I take it for granted that the bulk of the rebels were captured by them. A man with experience in roping a horse could rope four or five Negroes with one try.

That was what ended the little war of '12 here. Let them say the Cuban officers did their job, alright, let them. I'll put my hands in a flame if the Americans weren't the real saviors.

On the 24th of June, 1912, Evaristo Estenoz was killed. It was St. John's day, that's why I remember it so clearly.

The death of the ringleader finished off the insurrection. I returned to Havana with the old man when train service was resumed again. I bought the newspaper and saw a cartoon that gave the key to understand that binge. It was in the *Political Funnies*.

Two bumpkins wearing tropical shirts and straw hats were saying:

> In Cuba's rich and happy nation,
> Bigshots too feed chicks their ration.

And you could see a field general in a corner, with a bag in one hand and a sword in the other, tossing corn to a flock of crows. Who knows if it's true that the Negroes received any money? No one. It stayed that way. And the ones who sacrificed themselves were the ones who followed the leaders, Estenoz and Ivonet.

> Here you all have Ivonet
> A dark skinned Frenchie Cuban,
> Put this land in a tourniquet,
> 'Cause he's the rebel's chieftain.
> He sports the Haitian uniforms
> Of general 'n commander,
> And soon he'll be forsworn
> To serve as our defender.

And the other couplet was dedicated to Evaristo. I can't forget it because I sang it a lot for fun:

> That valiant general
> Black and independent
> Proclaimed himself President

And now Emperor Tropical;
To see him so weighty
In his bright uniform
We must promptly inform
You: Why, this must be Haiti!

Just as I said, after the war, a little music.
Of course, there was no one who could replace the blood.
Stars of gold, boots with silver spurs, rough cotton drill pants . . .
I should say! No country could put up with a war like that.
The Negroes were smashed for being ambitious and racist.

And what the hell did they think, that we were going to turn ourselves in like little lambs, that we were going to put down our weapons and pull down our pants? Not at all. And we showed them. They called us savages, little patent leather boys and a thousand other insults, but since when in this country has a program more democratic than that of the Independents of Color been brought before the people than when we fought tooth and nail to gain benefits for us Negroes, who had come out of the war barefooted and in rags, hungry, just like Quintín Banderas, who was killed later while he was getting water from the well in his house? Let's not hear any more cheap talk. The moment of justice has arrived. And none of us who risked our necks in that little war are going to keep our mouths closed.

Anyway, whoever comes here where I stand and talks about racism, saying that the Negroes were bloodthirsty, I'm going to give him a punch in the nose so he'll know who Esteban Montejo is.

I don't know what the journalists, the writers, and the politicians think about that. But as for me, as a man, as a

58

citizen and as a revolutionary, I think that it was a just struggle. With its egotism and its errors, but necessary. The Negroes didn't have anything to cling to, they couldn't even breathe and they had been generals and men of letters, like Juan Gualberto Gómez. I'm not interested in what that woman says. I see things from another perspective. I knew her and she liked the good life, never had a social concern, or was interested in national politics. She did her little shows there and then she'd go home much pleased with herself. Do you believe that can be given value? In my mind what she says about the Negroes' insurrection is pure foolishness. A racist woman like her, opportunistic and . . . Better not to go into that. I declare my admiration for those men who tried to breathe freely. And if she says they're animals or were animals, I'm not concerned. She was the animal that took advantage of this Republic, that only knew how to accumulate wealth. Because she didn't have fame, much less glory. Rachel is the best example of the prostitution, the vice and the lie wrapped in a red ribbon that reigned in this country. I say that and I affirm it. And as far as I know, I don't have a single drop of Negro blood. But I see things as they are, as they have to be. Listen to her, because she's nice, fun-loving, and she knows some trifles, but don't pay much attention. I'm telling you this and I've been plugging along in life for quite some time now.

The sad thing is that the circus folded up. Now to look for new directions. And carrying the old man on my back.

I got to Havana and went to see my two loves: Mama first of all, and then my dear Adolfo.

I found Mama down in the mouth. And Adolfo in the same cloud as always: "Rachel, now it looks like things are going to go better."

That numbskull had faith in the least generous people who ever walked the planet.

I had to cheer up two creatures who didn't have anyone else in the world but this poor devil, me, the one who's sad, the one who's collapsed, me, the dummy.

The old man set me up in a room so I could live alone. And that's how it turned out. I lived alone because after two or three months I gave him the gate, and I wasn't going to give up my room, was I?

"I'm going to kill myself. I'll throw myself into the sea."

"Go ahead," I said to him, "commit suicide, but don't come to ask me for anything more."

Crying, I packed a change of clothes in a bag and watched him go defeated. I'm sorry. That man was a droop and, young and in love, I wasn't going to carry that gruesome weight around my whole life. He helped me, but I made the circus for him and a lot of other things. I did my part, I'd say, being of sane mind. The room turned out pretty because Adolfo decorated it with some pale blue lace curtains. He fixed up my bed in the imperial style, with some little pale flowers too, that were admired by all who saw them. Painted by hand and given a patina. We covered the walls with Austrian scenes: stags, rams, little country houses . . .

On the headboard of my bed, I put up a precious gold medallion with the face of Janus, which has a sad side and another one that smiles at life. It's the symbol of the theater all over the world.

I finally succeeded in having a corner to myself. I received many friends there, why should I deny it? They helped me pay for my expenses until I managed to get on my feet.

The old man appeared two or three months later and said:

"You're a whore like your saintly mother."

I closed the door in his face, with a slam, and I didn't say a word . . . I did good, I did good.

White, very white, beautiful, very beautiful and elegant, with lovely eyes, black and oval, with a haughty presence, an enchanting smile and a little foot like an almond.

The Gay Theater, Santiago, Cuba, 1912

Chapter Four

On the street again, with no place to stay. But ready to face everything head on.

Now it's true, I would never go back to a circus like that one. I killed the afternoons walking around. All of Prado Park, the Plaza de Marte, Payret Park, that was my zone of operations. I was a free woman who could carry on my own business. I missed the clamor of the theater, my world, what I was born for, but I knew how to apply control. I waited two years without moving a finger, living from "souvenirs," without promises to anybody and free from Mama. Lots of adventure, night life, alcohol, parties, little strolls. But not a thing artistic. I went to all the theaters of that period, as a spectator. I'd sit with a friend in a good seat, always front row and watch the show. Those were the years of Monterito, Pastor, Chelito Criolla . . . I observed them carefully. Not to imitate them but to collect things, out of spite. They all had some defect. The one who wasn't cock-eyed was dumb. The one who wasn't dumb was too slutty. The other one was very fat or very ugly like Chelito. The one on this side, pretentious. The one over there, absent-minded.

They were all in a minor key. That's why I was so convinced of my talent.

The best proof of my quality was in those others, the mirror where I looked at myself like in the story of Snow White.

I'd come home and lie down on the bed to practice pretending. I bought a mirror on Dragones street. A standing mirror with two beautiful ancient Greek style columns. I put it in front of the bed to see myself anytime. All by myself I studied all the gestures and expressions an entertainer ought to know. I'd make an effort to smile and then laugh heartily. I cried like a Magdelene, smoked like a bandit, let myself get carried away, sobbed and then recited Becerra's monologues from Pous' company of strolling buffoons, or *bululú*. I did over again all I had done at the Tivoli and in the circus. That was daily. I surpassed myself on my own.

I have to be very grateful to Adolfo, that's true, but even without him I would have been who I was.

Together we bought a phonograph and, happy like crazy, we'd do our own performances. I would dance till I dropped and, passing out, he followed every step.

Here goes the Conga of the Negress:

> I'm the Black girl Tomasa,
> Flower of Joseph 'n Mary.
> Don't call on me vulgarly
> Don't want no showing off-ah
> No handsome man who goes to far-ah
> 'Cause I'm a real good looker too,
> A loose cigar in a skirt
> So whoever wants a taste of me,
> I tell him so saucily:
> Don't play with fire, don't get burnt.

And the rhetorical one, who talked like a college student:

> I am Concepción Baró
> Philosophy's my cup o' tea
> And to my heart the very key,
> Believing in Mary and Joe.
> I don't know what a rumba is,
> nor the conga or a danzón.

I'm Christian by religion
So if fooling around's your plan
Know for sure that this mulatta
Won't swish her skirts for any man.

The fun is in knowing how to act the different types. The mulatta conga is the one without polish, the primitive one. A woman with a shawl and rings. She wears sandals, sells rolls or flowers but the rhetorical one, no, she most likely wears full skirts, speaks quietly, pronounces her s's, wears glasses, irons the kinks out of her hair every day and reads, a rare thing among colored women.

I find myself in the middle of these tenements, making like a social worker, or a school inspector. Chummy with the most low life Negroes, all to record in detail the customs of those slums, the way the Negro women talked, moved, danced. I became a sponge. That's why the mulatta I brought to the Cuban theater made history. They tried to imitate her but they all failed.

It was a war to the death for me. A performer succeeds once she manages to portray a character.

The mediocre ones are those who don't know how to do either a mulatta, a Chinese woman, or Death. Those are the ones who later sabotage things and show their nails. Even though they might be under the ground, I'll identify them one of these days by name and address because they made life impossible for me. Impossible!

They would come into the dressing rooms to insult me, they believed I was the devil's daughter. They tore up my music, they burned my clothes, they prejudiced the bosses, the stage hands, the set designers against me. They made my life impossible:

"Rachel is a bitch."

"Rachel is a whore."

"Rachel is hoarse."

"She's got bony legs, she's a lesbian. Get her out of here because she cheapens the name of the theater. Put her in the chorus. Throw her into a cess pool to see if she'll disappear."

I'm going to name them one by one along with their defects and then we'll see who's right. We'll see.

Our relationship was all balcony to balcony. She'd peer out in the afternoons and I would too and we'd say some silly things across the way, signals, gestures more like.

She watched people with a lot of curiosity but didn't say hello to anyone.

"Rachel, how are you today?"

And always tipsy and happy, she'd open her left hand and that meant really fine.

Rachel is a little hypocrite. She plays the recluse so she'll be pampered. She's always lived for praise, though she may have cloistered herself up like a nun since '39 or '40, since she left the Alhambra Theater. She closed herself in with her dog and her maid and her mother, an old Hungarian woman who was really something else. They say she was the one who introduced "the mother tongue" in San Isidro. She was an old featherbrain who spent her life talking about her daughter's triumphs: "My little girl, my little girl was, my little girl this, and my little girl that."

I know, I've seen from paintings she has in the house that she was a real woman. About her art, well . . . as with all things, a little leavening. Now, there's no question when it comes to the part about being a woman. Big breasted with large, round hips. If I were a novelist, I'd write a portrait of that woman, a la Zola, or Flaubert, but here I stay in disgusting misery with a demolished idea and I think no novel's ever going to come out of me, not even if it wants to.

Well, her face wasn't marvelous: little Jewish parrot beak of a nose and jumpy eyes, quite expressive, black, long eyebrows. Jetblack hair and . . .

Balcony to balcony or on the phone, because she's never let me touch even her finger, nothing. She's a very private woman.

One night, by chance, I hit it off with the maid, and she had me up to the house, on account of lust, and I went. With a tiny light, I saw the living room and a closed bedroom. Ofelia, nervous, pointed:

"That's where the lady sleeps, be quiet."

We had cognac, Ofelia and I. A bottle with gold netting and it tasted glorious, thick and a little warm.

Poor Rachel, she was a bit of a drinker, and so she wouldn't allow herself to be seen, because of her tell-tale breath.

She says, well it's said, that she used to go to church, to the confessional to confess her sins, women's foolishness, and that she had Ofelia talk as if she were her.

Ofelia faced the priest and answered and prayed in Rachel's name.

She knew the lady's whole life and glory, so she could lend herself to the farce. I can't understand all those little secret crannies of hers because the priests at this point drink like demons and their breath reeks more than Bacchus's.

One night Adolfo shows up dressed as a geisha. He nearly knocks the door down.

"Let's go, get dressed, we are on the high road now."

"But, what's going on?"

"Rachel, we're going to the Parraga's house, it's an opportunity for you."

When he said it was an opportunity, I saw a star shine in the firmament. Those months of the summer of 1914 I haven't ever been able to forget. My friend, a lawyer with money, had died on me a few weeks before on account of a bubonic plague we'd had in Cuba. I was left without a penny. If it hadn't been for Adolfo and that night, my life would have taken a fatal direction.

I dressed for a gala occasion. I say that instead of saying like a queen. I played the part of a 20-year-old, no older. Authentically 20 years old. Because there are women who at 20 walk around decked out to show off that they're 20, and that's an error. At 20, no excesses, none of that costume jewelry. That was me. Lips lightly painted, cheeks shaded with scandalous pink, eyelids well lined in the Chinese manner, oval shaped and sensual, hair apparently unkempt but with a lot of shine, impeccable nails, certainly, long and pink, a grey rose color, torso erect with a very fine Venetian mother-of-pearl necklace and a *chatrés* dress tucked in at the waist and very full at the bottom. I never liked to take handbags to parties even though it was the fashion. Your hands should have their own independence. Handbags and junk like rings, bracelets and the rest are an obstacle. Instead of contributing, they detract.

The Parragas are the owners of a sugar plantation and like hand and glove with the President. They had built a big house on Línea street, which in those days was like saying a meandering river. The house was luxurious but ugly. It had the look of a toad: a bulky, rounded facade, many columns and a side stairway that lead to the north terrace. It was there I arrived after a long ride in the car. The party began at 7:30. The commotion was horrible. The times had changed. More money was coming into the country. It was the beginning of the so-called Dance of the Millions, the Fat Cows, to give it another name.

The Parragas didn't know me, but Adolfo had arranged to speak to the lady of the house and she, who saw right through him, said yes: "Have her come and dance and sing and do whatever she wants. This is a democratic house. We're art lovers. Bring her and we'll see if she's pleasing."

The rich are self-centered, capricious, they abuse an entertainer. I say that without rancor. Not one of them found my weak spot, but they did make me swallow bile a couple of

67

times. The saddest thing for an entertainer is to sing or dance at a private party. The guests, in their lechery, don't pay attention. They drink and drink and they don't even notice you. I say they never found my weak spot but they did make me suffer. I did no more there than enter and immediately all eyes were devouring me to see how to get the best slice from the ham.

I did what I had to do. I sang two or three *guarachas*, I danced and declaimed a mulatta's monologue I knew by heart. They sprinkled champagne and French and Bulgarian liqueurs.

"They didn't hear me, they didn't even realize, they don't even know my name."

"No, girl, don't worry, you'll soon see they do."

That rascal knew more than a weasel. A short while later a man with thick sideburns, dressed in fine linen and with a clean smell, tall and very meticulous, approached me.

"Miss, will you give me a dance?"

"Yes, certainly."

We danced around a good stretch of the hall. We drank. I almost forgot I had come escorted by Adolfo. The man took me out on the balcony and laid on the flattery. Being well habituated and used to it, I didn't pay the least bit of attention to him. The most he managed to do was hold my hand and recite some of his poems that he carried in a tiny Chinese paper envelope. Nothing more.

Later, the party continued and I asked Adolfo to go outside with me to the garden to get some fresh air. The Parragas chased me, the old lady insisting. "Have her dance and sing again. Girl, don't be like this, be pleasant, life is short . . ."

She made me not want to budge. Sing, not a bit of it. One of those old ladies who ragged on.

We went into the hall and there he is, leaning on the glass of the door waiting for me.

"Who is that young man?"

"My agent."

"Your agent?"

"Yes, the one who guides me and cheers me on."

"Ah!"

"Rachel, I want to see you Saturday morning in my office. I am an impresario of an important theater. What do you think?

My hands got stuck together as if they were magnets and I couldn't say thanks or hello because even my tongue had gone stiff. But Adolfo, who was ready for whatever dropped, ran over and initiated a long conversation with Federico, the impresario.

We stars know how to be indifferent and even transform timidity into sideways glances. He certainly believed I was a disdainful woman and that name or position weren't important to me. But he was wrong because there I was, seeing the sky clearly, more clearly than ever, trembling, transpiring, skittish. A woman of good judgement ought to know how to control her emotions and when she doesn't know what to say, she should remain discretely silent. I say and I repeat, "girls, don't scatter yourselves all about, learn the lesson of an old lady who, with cleverness and tenacity, has done everything in her life that her fantasy asked."

But no, they don't hear anybody, they're thick.

On the ground, like little chickens, on the ground and pounded into dirt! That's how I see them!

And if you don't believe me, look at the young people, with television, radio programs: parrots in a cage, voices of frogs, bulls, and the bodies of locusts. And if that weren't all, with no charm, climbing out of the dung, those are today's performers.

Rachel's face was very beautiful, as we've already said, although it would be more fair to say it was very beautiful, except when at rest.

When she was still, you discovered all of a sudden, with no little surprise, that her nose was excessively long and

pointed, *her mouth a bit tired and puerile, and her eyes
overly lacking in expression. In sum, a woman who has not
been finished, transplanted from the small town circus and
absolutely incapable of establishing the least harmony
between the demands of her art, her appetites, her dreams
and the routine of her daily life.*

*Each one of these things was a world unto itself and the
battle between them would have shortly reduced a less
resistant face to idiocy or to frivolity.*

*The calling of art attracted her greatly, and yet the call
of love attracted her more often, at least, it's known that
even businessmen and senators of the Republic sent her
cultivated pearls and Colombian emeralds.*

An anonymous unpublished criticism

I rested hours and hours. My bed became a bad habit. I
didn't go out on the street not even to talk. Anxiety conquered
me, the urgency to do my own work and the waiting. I
awaited the visit of that man. Bastard!

Saturday, marked with a circle in China ink on the
calendar, had already passed. The man had interviewed me,
but before putting me to the most difficult test of my life,
trying out in a great theater, which was like saying jump
from the pan into the fire, he had informed me:

"A visit to your house, to talk, just the two of us. I'd have
to explain the conditions to you, it's not all so easy, Rachel,
there are others in the way, hundreds, and I want you to be on
solid ground."

How was I not going to believe him! He couldn't tell me
road stories or paint storm clouds for me. I was already more
fearless than the devil himself and nothing was going to
convince me that didn't call a spade a spade.

That's why I told him yes, that he should come to my
house whenever he wished, preferably during daylight hours
because at night I went out to clear my head, with Adolfo,

with the gal from the slums, with Carmen, with the Gallician girl.

I rested fitfully, not just for hours, for days and even weeks. I didn't go out much because my nerves wouldn't let me. The sun, the heat, the lack of air, everything . . . the waiting.

I practiced with new monologues. I combed all the theaters in the capitol, even the dives on the plaza: floor tiles badly placed and platforms almost on ground level, those were the sets of the dancers I saw and it pained my heart to think, my God, to think that I might have to go backward into those hell holes.

That's why I waited that way, because my soul would leap each time the street door squeaked, or someone scratched it or Adolfito arrived with his childish games.

"Calm down, woman. Calm down."

"I'm tired, I'm getting tired of waiting."

"I'm telling you he's going to come the day you least expect. He remembers you."

"What did he tell you?"

"That you have courage."

"Courage yes, but no talent."

"Be quiet, don't be a child. To have courage means that you can give the best of yourself and that he has confidence in you."

"Isn't it probably that other thing . . ?"

"What?"

"That other thing, you know, don't be sly."

"No, Rachel, Federico has a wife and is an impresario not a pimp."

"Ay! Mariana Grajales, I beg you. Let me begin to work in this theater! Marianita, I beg of you!"

Those anguished days forced me, I don't know, they said to me, take paper and pencil and write. It's not that I wanted to be a writer or poetess. No sir! I was far from that but I took a satchel of papers and I considered writing some pages that

71

afterward remained engraved from my saying them so much, to myself, because I never recited even a single verse to Adolfo.

I wrote and wrote like a crazy woman and then I'd keep the pages under my night table, not even in the drawer, so nobody would just happen on them someday.

What do I feel while writing? What did I feel, because never again have I taken up a pencil.

Well, I felt the world was marvelous and terrible, that I was alone and wished to express beautiful, sad things, my loneliness, my love, my art. Everything I had dreamed in my life, and the paper, poor thing, always responded, the paper didn't disappoint me, so I wrote, to fill the vacuum, exactly like when I rehearsed or made candy.

I filled sheet after sheet and didn't consider burning them up, I don't know if it's because I'm so proud, since deep down it seems to me that everything I do is well done no matter how poor it may be . . . The fact is that I still have them stored away along with some tortoise shell combs and a miniature porcelain that my aunt gave me on our trip to Vienna. Those are my memories and I keep them because I feel relief and melancholy when I touch them or see them.

They're the things a woman keeps and that are alive, that have been with her and that, why not confess it, are herself.

It pains me to speak so much about myself, about my intimate life. Much pain, I assure you.

Verses to Memory

> *For my friend and faithful companion*
> *Adolfo Estiró*

I remember that there in other clouds
a nightingale proclaimed life to me.
I remember butterflies murmuring,

72

sleeping beneath my weary brow
and I remember the instant ache of oblivion
when your hands stretched out to mine
to say goodbye, farewell, first
love that was, O torment and tempestuous
seas, and you tore from your throat
a shout, to wave a lonely adieu to this
fierce world and leave me adrift.
Goodbye love! Goodbye life!

Another devoted to art and written a little later. This is a sonnet or something like that. I will say the first verse and the last.

The last: Art, accompany me all the way to the grave.
The first: Art that awakens in me life . . .

I'm not a writer, I wasn't, I should say. I wrote those poems without ever having read a complete book of verse. Now I wish I had a most elegant volume Federico gave me a few days after signing me. I lost it in a dressing room quarrel. A whore grabbed it and stole it. That's how things are. Nevertheless, I remember it was a small blue book, very smooth, of the best leather and embossed in gold with ribbons and little circles. An exquisite book! The author was named Alfred Musset and he was French.

Even today I can recite by heart the first poem in the book, which didn't come on page one but on page nine, something that really caught my eye.

The verses said:

Poet, take your lute and give me a kiss.
Soon the buds of the wild rose
will open, and today in this land
spring is born: breezes become inflamed
and the thrush that the dawn has awakened

will perch in new foliage.
Poet, take your lute and give me a kiss.

Then came the poet's part because it was a duet between the muse and him. If one could only retain those things in one's memory it would be marvelous. To walk along the beach in the sand, along the breakwater, and repeat the verses. It would be a privilege to have a memory like that.

My word. My word of honor.
That was the door she came through.
And that's not slander, it's the truth in capital letters.
Many plays I wrote for that theater.
She saw the path, followed the little light, and came in. She knew what she was doing. Later they probably became envious of her, they probably whipped her, but it's the real truth. I would almost say that the Alhambra got to be as famous as it did because of her. The watchman at the Normal School knows the story well. He was a stagehand there. He knows that Rachel is not what the papers highlighted. What happens these days is that nobody tells it straight and since she's old and retired . . . Let her be. The short of it is, there have been lots of whores: Claudia, Cleopatra, Juliet, Aphrodite, they were all of the same stripe. There's a verse that says: Birds of a feather, fly together. I think it's Shakespeare, but I'm not sure.

My room filled up with flowers. Receiving different vases for twelve days: daisies, gladioli, Seville carnations, dahlias. Twelve days I spent on the verge of insanity. If I didn't end up all twisted it was due to my integrity and my faith. I said: "Rachel, you're not crazy. What you are is tormented, weak." And I put my finger up to my nose and I'd move it away to see if it didn't go off to one side and if my pulse responded. I would also take a glass and ask for water and I'd drink it sitting in bed, and I'd swallow and it was water I was drinking. That's to say, that I was in my right mind. But the doctors didn't have the same opinion. So I spent twelve days in the hospital. Mama and I made up. She asked the nurse in a low voice: "My little girl, she's not bad off, she'll be saved?" Me, hearing that, I thought, nope, what I've got is an internal hemorrhage, a cancer or something like that. The only one to hit it on the nail was Adolfo, who got me out of bed one day and said to me: "That's enough. I know you better than I know myself. Get up and walk. The only thing you have is that you're an artist and you're suffering because you feel wretched with nothing in life to excite you. Let's get out of here running, these people are going to kill you with those pills." How clear he saw it all!

With those words I got up and at three in the afternoon, Mama, Adolfo and I were waiting for a cab.

We got to my house in the cab and such a great relief filled me to see my wallpaper, my mirror, my flowers.

Adolfo let my hair down and began to make me some Recamier curls that weren't in style anymore but I put up with it out of friendship, which is worth more than anything in life . . .

I was stupid to let myself get carried away by nerves but if it weren't for that I wouldn't get into the Alhambra. Federico came to see me every day at my house. He kept on sending me flowers. The neighbors whispering: "That gal, what's she up to, she's going to ruin the man, soaks him dry, the poor wife," and things like that, because there's no enemy worse than a neighbor. There isn't!

And in short, the only thing he did was to fill the house with flowers, at first I mean, because over time he began to realize I was single, to call it that, and that no one paid for the room, the lights, the bills. Then he began to be generous. He was paying for everything. He gave me presents of perfume, handkerchiefs, articles of clothing . . . With an open account, he sent me to a Moorish peddler. The Moor visited me once a week and from him I supplied myself . . . silks, wools, linens, all kinds of things. I dressed like a grand dame, and Adolfo didn't lack for anything, of course, the poor boy. Federico was no dummy. He well knew that Adolfo was my right hand man, my confidant, and he began to use him to learn about my life. But me, who knows more than the mother who bore me, I turned into a little saint. Freddy here and Freddy there.

I tied him down like a rider does his horse. And no matter how many kicks he gave, he never left the ring. He was faithful to me for many years. And he protected me in the Alhambra Theater like a queen on her throne. I only cheated on him two times but I was made to do it. By my mother, by my mother!

Chapter Five

Every man is ashamed of his dream-stained face
Hadrian's *Memoirs*

All these papers are old. Any one of them is fifty years old, more. The album is recent, of interviews done after my retirement. I have it to show journalists, but the papers, the plays, the old photos, I don't know, sometimes I get the jitters and I think about putting them under lock and key and let any one dare. What for, I say, whoever sees them now probably doesn't know how to value them. So I lock them up.

They don't fit in the dresser anymore or in the bed side table.

This room, the house, everywhere, it's all piled up with things . . .

Between the papers, the dog, and Ofelia . . ! I'm going to have this piece of furniture in the anteroom made bigger because it's good mahogany, from the time of Columbus. I'm going to make some shelves up above to put the plays and the clippings on. The photos no, they're going in the box and in the drawers of the bed side table. This one from 1913 is ugly because it's lost its shine. This yellowing one is the one I like the most. Here I look like I am, happy and saucy, isn't that true? I hate this one with the small groups, there are always intruders. The one on the right is Federico, the one with the wire rimmed eye glasses. This one is Luz. How young she looks! And this one is Trías, a very pretty woman quite at ease with herself. I am truly ugly here, I have the face of a Jewess. It's not me, no way! It's better to tear up photographs or burn them. Mama was the one with the idea of collecting. An old European habit.

Here I'm alright. The mesh tights, a bit too snug, but my very likeness. *Fresh Meat*. Who could remember that! It was the name of the first comedy I did at the Alhambra. A pornographic man, that says it all. These are scripts in Federico's own handwriting. I'll read the dialogue from the first scene. You'll see what a play. Talent and spark, things the playwrights of today don't have.

Alright, I'll make an effort so it comes out good, but years are years and they don't pass in vain. Maybe my memory will fail or I'll skip a line, I ask you to excuse any slip, and I hope you don't get bored.

We're at a great masked ball. Music, punchinellos, harlequins, fauns, centaurs, half masks, gondoliers, sea nymphs, vampires, everything that makes a masked ball.

The hall quite lit up, wide, with two candelabra lamps hanging from the ceiling.

A couple named Alberto and Rosita enter.

They come simply dressed, she with a black half mask and he with another.

Alberto is graceful and young. Rosita, his wife, is young too but very ugly. The dance begins and everyone goes out to look for a partner.

To one side of the hall a very elegant young man lounges smoking with a long, mother-of-pearl cigarette holder. His name is Teodoro and he has entered the party incognito. He is haughty—a dandy, I would say. All the young women watch him discretely but he acts as if nothing was happening. He doesn't even speak. He gets up, runs his elegant hands over the grand piano and blows out a mouthful of smoke. Alberto and Rosita have danced the first piece and she stretches out on the divan to rest and to fan herself for a while.

Teodoro seizes the opportunity and addresses Alberto:

Teodoro: I'm sure you don't remember me.

Alberto: I don't, to tell the honest truth.

Teodoro: Try to remember.

Alberto: No matter how much you insist, I don't know you sir.

Teodoro: Traitor, liar, let's get out of here!

(*They head toward the garden.*)

They exit hurriedly. Teodoro's lips tremble. Alberto, swiftly, goes toward an encounter of hand to hand combat.

The garden fills up with fireflies according to the taste of the set designer.

Teodoro gives Alberto a kiss on the lips and repeats his question.

Teodoro: Tell me now you don't know who I am.

Alberto: Magdalena, my life, what are you doing here, and in that get up? For the love of God, if they see us.

Teodoro: I love you Alberto, I have come to get you. You know I would do unspeakable things for you; I'm not saying I would dress up as a man, but as a tart, as a Gypsy, whatever, in order to be by your side for a moment.

Alberto: My Magdalena, the love you offer me is undeserved. My mind is ruined and my hopes are dead. I am a river where all human excretions accumulate. Get you away, my murky waters can no longer be purified in you. It's too late.

Teodoro: (*Fearfully, and placing his hands on his head.*) No, my love, there is time yet, the night awaits us, let's flee from this cheap world.

They kiss frantically. The fireflies gradually turn off their tremulous light. There is a silence and then a shout of horror.

Curses! Betrayal! I'll kill you, traitor!

It's Rosita, who, when she discovers the scene, screams to vent her emotions. The dancing stops and the two lovers, in the middle of the hall, are attacked for public indecency. Rosita, listless, asks to be burned at the stake.

Teodoro, his hands up in the air, pleads to the audience for a moment of silence.

Teodoro: A misunderstanding. A misunderstanding.

Alberto asks her to undress and Teodoro begins to take off pieces of clothing before the horrified eyes of the guests at the masked ball.

Magdalena de Maupin is completely nude. Her blond hair falls softly over her shoulders, her bare bosom projects gracefully and so, each light is turned off until there remains the young and beautiful Magdalena de Maupin, played by myself, in an oasis of light, under the thunderous applause of the audience of the Alhambra Theater. That was my opening. Tell me if I didn't come in through the front door!

Miss Maupin, please come out.
And she paraded, wearing her skin colored tights, her blond hair reaching to her waist.
In that chorus of grannies, Rachel was the spoiled little girl.
Miss Maupin, and I, the curtains open and close.
Miss Maupin . . . and finally she'd come out again, give a peek at her breasts and that was her ancor.
Miss Maupin, but since she didn't sing . . .

Rachel "The Bauble"

The other day I was introduced to her, an honor that allowed me to know up close the new starlet at the Alhambra, for whom I have always felt a great deal of affection.

Rachel, who is at the top of her form, is the soul of the Alhambra and performs with exquisite taste, and when she sings, her voice makes one forget life's cares.

I, who only on occasion go to the theater, will in future be an assiduous patron of the pleasant Coliseum of the Virtues.

This actress has a very fine quality, not common among show people, which is that she performs with the same gusto, though there may only be four spectators in the audience.

With great pleasure I dedicate these lines to her and I wish her great success in her challenging artistic work.

Nolo de Lin,
The Gay Theater,
Weekly Review,
Havana

No sooner did I put my foot on that stage than I began to see everything upside down. As if I had been taken by the hair, like this and put on my head. The world for me became more complicated or more complete. A world that was more than a world, it was a puzzle.

Before, I hadn't had experiences like the ones I had at the Alhambra. Everything happened to me there. It was a steam cooker, about that we'll always be in agreement, that part doesn't have to be made into a fantasy, but in that steamer you gained in all the senses.

For me, who knew the good and the bad of life, who wasn't a little child any more, it didn't change me to the point of making me different, but it sure did open my eyes to life, to art, and to you, villainous men, which is the most useful lesson a woman can learn.

From the time I arrived, I can say from the first day, I was everybody's spoiled child, except for the cockatoos. Those ladies readied the guillotine for me, but in vain, it was totally in vain, because look at me here with my little mother-of-pearl necklace, with . . .

Young men brought flowers to my dressing room: doctors, lawyers, authors, a group I had that carried my name. You should have heard Luz: "Look, there's the gang—she didn't say sympathizers, admirers, none of that, Rachel's *gang*. She said it with rage, with the worst kind of jealousy, because, beautiful and all, she never brought together so many men. She lacked attractiveness and poise. Mexicans are like that, thick blood. Not the Cuban girl. She can wiggle through the eye of a needle. So much so that I can say openly that the greatest number of plays Federico wrote after the period I first appeared there were written especially for my key. And that is a privilege. I say it isn't the same to act in a play in the abstract, which is the same for a fatty as for a stick, as it is to act in one directed for a particular voice, a style, a body. It's not the same. That's why I can be proud of myself. In such and such a play there was a queen, she was me. There was an aristocratic lady, she was me. There was a sexy lady, she was me and so, me, me, me. All but the dumb little country gal or the homebody, the modest one, wearing a perm and tidy calico dresses!

The Alhambra was a finishing school. The girl who entered came out a woman. In Havana's dives the girls would lose their stirrups, begin to whore around right away, show their thighs in the first shows, wouldn't arouse the men, they'd become a little crazy, and they'd ruin the charm.

On account of that, because I knew those theaters, where there wasn't anybody who could direct, I was enthusiastic about getting in at the Alhambra. The impresarios there keep an eye on morality, up to where it was their business, of course. They didn't allow the chorus girls to receive men in their dressing rooms, unless it was a well heeled gentleman or a politician. They had to call us Miss and Ma'am. None of that listen girl, hey you, none of that.

Morality was the basis for the success of a performer at the Alhambra, the same in my case as for a third row chorus girl.

The key point for why I say that the Alhambra was a school was politics. Anything that caused a buzz in the country passed through the Alhambra. A scandalous murder.

82

There went so and so or what's his name and wrote a script. A coup d'etat, the Americans wanted to steal the island, a bandit was getting away with murder, and so on. That was the Alhambra. As I say: a sieve. Besides that, the classics were loved. The life of the Greeks in Athens, of the Romans, the battle of Waterloo, the blind love of Abelard and Heloise or Romeo and Juliette, the passion for the automobile, jealousy, all the feelings of an educated person were reflected in the plays of the Alhambra. That's why you learned a lot and at first hand. We didn't want clumsy women there. Vivacious women, rotten ones, with their vinegar, arrogant, that certainly wasn't looked down on, but a little dimwit, on the street in two seconds. A performer at the Alhambra had to be up to date and have her faculties sharp. If not, she failed. She failed because the authors said: "You have to be on our level. Read and interpret. Don't learn things by rote." And that was what I did. One play I even dared to criticize and give it a different meaning. I'm bold, aren't I?

But that was what put me on a first name basis with the writers. They could say Rachel has overacted, Rachel exaggerates, but never did a single one say that Rachel didn't understand the script. Never that.

In Madame Maupin, at the beginning, for lack of experience, I followed the dialogue word for word. But later on, I added all the ad libs I felt like, elevating the work, making that puny script a work of quality.

I'm going to take a chance and this has to be secret. I'm going to say something that would be classed as heresy. The actresses at the Alhambra, me in particular, we made the plays, we enriched them. We were the yeast and thanks to us the authors triumphed. Sometimes what they had written was the biggest piece of shit in the world. I have the nerve to say this. But be very careful, because they're probably coming after me with clubs and I'm already old.

Alright, what the hell! Da truth forever more.

. . . and later they'll call us "Indians in tuxes" when we have shown we know what art is by carrying Rachel triumphantly on our shoulders.

Theatrical intrigues, that make up the drama behind the scenes, haven't found an echo in Rachel, who appears to have always skipped over poorly disguised envy, like the bird of the verse "without having sullied her plumage."

For the triumphant one of yesterday, today and tomorrow go these lines I have been permitted to translate from the book of reality.

Cesar Ocampo, The Gay Theater,
Havana

Already on an even keel more or less, I decided to move from my little room. Federico supported the plan. The neighbors wouldn't leave us alone. They threw witchcraft in the doorway: chickens, tiny red bananas wrapped in old rags, black copper pennies, every imaginable thing!

We moved, or better said, I moved to Campanario street, to the windy heights that overlooked the sea. I'd look and make out like I were travelling on a transatlantic liner. Havana was very pretty, prettier than today, because there was tranquility. The ocean in front of my house, the waves, El Morro nearby, the breakwater wall, the peanut vendors, almost always Chinese. My Havana at night time was a fair. To walk, to walk was my thing, my hobby, not collecting stamps, or biscuit dolls, that always seemed idiotic to me. To walk till you're worn out and to talk with friends. A conversation about love is worth an entire life. It's what I miss, for Mama's sake. My life now doesn't have any meaning. I am sad, alone, bewildered. Oh!

But all of this is like falling over a cliff. No. I'm a woman of temperament, I'm not dramatic, I've already said so and I repeat it. I'm a woman who knows how to always come out afloat. Like buoys, so the young guys come and sink them and the buoys, rise up again, pop!

I was saying that I moved. That's right. The move stimulated me. Federico himself helped me carry the miniatures and a trunk or two. I was already well established in the theater and I said to myself: "Mama and Adolfo are going to see the sky full of colors now. They've been pretty well screwed. They've been through a lot of suffering and I have a duty to help them." I took Mama with me. The old lady got used to my ways. But Adolfo refused to come. When he told me no, my body went cold.

He had his own independence and I respected it. I gave him money and continued to see him at night in the fresh air of the Prado.

Adolfo had a woman friend there who played the contrabass in the Alvarez Sisters' orchestra. She was short and, out of charity, he helped her with her instrument. "You're a shrewd one," he said. He wanted to let me live alone because he was so jealous he couldn't tolerate any of my friends. But what I'm getting to, the blackest day of my life, the 13th of August, 1916. 13, which is itself a macabre number.

I began to arrange the furniture: two or three old pieces I had, the ancient Greek mirror, the armoire, the secretary, two or three trifles. And like a dope, like a bull, I knock over the mirror with a thread of the mop and it breaks into pieces. I felt that my body was immediately a block of ice, my hands became stiff and I cried hysterically, in horror.

I'm not a pious woman, but I have my beliefs, I'm superstitious. And seeing that mirror on the floor smashed to bits, I said: "With my luck, someone is dying." That night I didn't sleep, I didn't want to frighten Mama, but I didn't sleep.

I felt that from one moment to the next, the news would come. I closed my eyes and it was worse. Finally, there was a knock at my door, at three or three thirty in the morning. I got up and breathed deeply to gather my energies.

I got to the door with my heart in my mouth. I opened it:

"You're the one who works at the Alhambra?"

"I am."

"Pardon the bother, miss, but I have to tell you something."

"Go ahead."

"Adolfo is in very serious condition in the Emergency Room."

"An accident?"

"No, Rachel. He was stabbed. It isn't known who. It isn't known."

"Is he alive?"

"I already told you he was in serious condition."

That word serious sounded very ugly to me. My legs went weak and right away got stronger again. I'm like that, in a tragedy I take control of myself.

When I got to the hospital I saw they were carrying a cadaver in a basket out through the back door. I approached the car and asked the man.

"A young man who died from a stabbing," he told me.

I paid for everything: funeral, layout, clothes . . . I closed his eyes and cried because I had lost a brother. But that night I performed, even with that and all. Of course, when I finished work I wasn't myself. I was a human rag. I was totally dejected.

Death is a bitch, right?

We've lived in a lion's den, in a cave of gangsters, in an anthill. We've been saved by a miracle, but that's how it was. I can't recall a happy childhood. I'm not complaining, but neither can I say like some: "Oh, my house, oh my parties, the piñatas, the trips, the car, etc, etc."

For us life had to be watched carefully. That's why nothing escaped us, not the good, not the bad. We're cured of fear. Not everything at the Alhambra started out well. The first test was a test by fire. I had to show that I was a headliner and that I didn't make concessions. Blanche helped me because she'd been there for years. She was pretty domesticated, a star with a large audience but she had no personal attractiveness.

I never tried to overshadow her. She did, with me. When she saw that I was who I was, she stopped coaching me. It didn't hurt me but we cooled off to each other. I already had my fans and the others couldn't swallow that so easily. The only pure, altruistic, loyal actress, the only human actress was me. But that's how it is. They treated me pretty badly, pretty damn bad.

When I started at the Alhambra, a bunch of gangsters gets unleashed on Havana. They sneak into the theater and begin to get away with murder. What a misfortune! It couldn't have been worse even if I'd dragged my own bad luck along. Everyday a different commotion. With bottle throwing, Bronx cheers, whistles, that's how the shows ended. They threw pennies at the performers who were real bad, to discredit them. The penny was a symbol of the most abusive thing. The gangs were called redskins. I don't know why that name, but I imagine it was for those Indians in the early movies who carved people up, shot poisoned arrows, all those tricks. The fact is that the redskins and I were always on good terms.

A redskin who was, usually, a newspaper peddler, or a shoe shine boy, or a cheap pimp, would show up and come to an agreement with a performer. For example, "Give me so much and when you come out on stage you'll get applause from more than thirty of us." If the performer was unknown she had to pay him the money so they would clap for her. That's how bribery was. And if So and So didn't pay or didn't want to make a deal, they'd wait for her at the stage door and slit her thigh like you'd cut a milk custard.

Many lost slices of their anatomy in that push and shove. But I repeat, they never bothered me. Blanca, Luz and I, we didn't need the red skins. The audience clapped for us with joy. I'd go out to sing a *guaracha* and the place would be up for grabs. Blanquita the same thing, and with Luz no doubt about it. But a poor girl who'd just started couldn't make a claim on the audience's soul, she had to go along with the bribes, that is if she wanted to know what applause was. I consider that to be a vexation, but on God's earth you can find anything, anything at all.

One night—the redskins had been pacified because the police were going around looking for them with black jacks—I go out really happy to do the 11 o'clock show. I made myself up pretty, very pretty, and I went out. Immediately, an ovation. I danced and sang a *guaracha* by Sánchez de Fuentes that came out to a tee. They turned on the lights, turned them off, opened the curtains, closed them, well, the audience was almost exhausted. I excited the men to such a point, I say it without modesty, but in the middle of all that I feel a penny fall into my cleavage. I almost changed colors. I looked at the audience and saw that everyone had realized it. I couldn't figure out what to do. I broke into a cold sweat. Finally, very delicately, I took that humiliation from between my breasts and like someone who has a gardenia in his hand, I kissed the penny and threw it back to the audience.

That gesture of mine was historic in the Alhambra. I had to sing that *guaracha* four times, with a thousand variations that came out spontaneously, moved by the applause. In the theater they called me the ragamuffin, the scamp, the brainy one. I gave a lesson without ever having that experience, that craftiness, without getting completely involved in that wicked game, because I was never any other thing but a big child about all that.

A poet says that performers are big children and that's as true as church. We are big children. We let ourselves be carried away by innocence, to such a point that triumph doesn't mean vanity, egotism, nothing like that for us. We're gifted with a thing called an angel, and with that we can die. And don't come to tell me now that an actress' career is ended when she retires. To be a performer isn't standing up on a stage and singing. It's feeling different than everyone else, loving with passion, hating with passion, feeling, which is so strange in the human species. That is a legitimate entertainer. Nobody has to come and put me on a pedestal. I'm grateful to the journalists for their attention, their cordiality, but they never discovered anything new. The performer in me was always there, will be there in the other life, because I tell you I'm going to dazzle the big shot angels. You don't think I can introduce a new tune standing at the right hand of God? Provided He doesn't send me to Purgatory!

When did you start in the theater?
As a child, I was almost a child.
What is it you like most in life?
To love with passion is the greatest thing there is. Then, good music, perfume; everything else is secondary.
If you weren't Rachel, who would you have liked to have been?
Francesca Bertini, Isidora Duncan, or myself in Paris.
What is your favorite stone?
Onyx and chalcedony, which I've never seen, but it's my birth stone.
Your color?
The color of the sky at seven in the evening. A pale reddish color.
What do you aspire to in your theatrical work?
That my audience acclaims me. And to live from art, decently, without having to ask anyone for a favor.
Who is the most influential person in your life?
Three people have been influential in my life. My mother, a friend who was like a brother to me, and my husband, Federico, because he's helped me to get ahead.
The newspaper La Lucha, February, 1924

Well, he was never the man who made me happy. Never. To be with him was a social pleasure for me. He stimulated me greatly but he didn't gratify me. Many times I had to grit my teeth to go to bed with him. Other times not, because since we both liked to go out after the show and have a few drinks in the theater bars, by the time we went to do that we were in a state of inebriation.

Then I didn't feel a thing. He'd touch me, he'd roll around, he'd bite me, and for me, nothing. Woman that I am, after all is said and done.

Many of those who went there were really good looking, men in their youth, dark, well groomed. They were my perdition.

Federico, so accustomed to see me with young men, wasn't jealous. He was intelligent at all times. If he hadn't been I would have jilted him. But he knew how to understand me. Deep down I still love him, with no pity, but yes with a little bit of guilt on my part. Once, and this shouldn't be known, for God's sake, a really handsome, intelligent young man comes to my dressing room and says to me: "Rachel, accept this."

He gives me some little bunches of forget-me-nots and he returns and he returns. He had me crazy. If I don't do something with him I'm going to become unhinged. He was studying medicine and his name was Pedro Carreño. Federico realizes all about my infatuation. I was cold with him. I didn't talk to him. I almost couldn't concentrate on my work. We weren't doing anything in bed. Until one night, when I went on stage like a crazy woman and I even lost the sense of the play by looking in the first rows to see if Pedro was there, as in fact he was. He was in the fourth row.

He no sooner saw me than he threw me a kiss. At the end of the performance, Federico came to see me and very quietly told me that he was going home alone, that because I needed something that wasn't exactly his company, he was going to let me be. I gave him a kiss on the forehead and said to him sadly: "Thank you, my life."

The young man was waiting outside. He approached me right away and he gave me a boutonniere he had. I myself said "let's go." I had the devil inside my body. I never enjoyed going to bed with a man so much. He smelled of cologne and I was perfumed too. That was the living end. First we kissed tenderly, as things always begin. Then I remember he asked me to take off my blouse. I didn't take it off and he came and unbuttoned me. When a woman makes love she always gets nervous no matter how much of the world she's seen. At that moment I felt like crying because I had fulfilled a great big desire.

Marks remained on my entire body, but I found release. There is nothing in life that can bring more pleasure than a moment of lust like that. Later we saw each other several times and some of those were pretty steamy, but never, ever, like that night.

Youth is a treasure. And two passionate young people in a bed are worth a whole life. I don't comprehend spinsters, or widows who stay single, or nuns, or even priests themselves. I will never comprehend them. For me they're abnormal, truncated people. Oh, men! How I need them!

Again last night I had the same nightmare as the other day. It's a baby dressed in white, squat and thicker than not. You don't see him very clearly but he's probably pretty, because he has green eyes, which are the only things that show up as if they were coming out of his face. At first it scared me a lot. Not now. Now I concentrate and let him pass by. He goes around the whole room, floating, and carries a couple of sheets of paper with musical notations in his hand. He comes up to me, after having gone two or three times around the bed and he hands the paper over to me. Then he lifts the hair from my forehead and gives me a kiss. It's not that the child is in love with me, because I'm a girl and little angels aren't interested in that, but when he kisses me I feel happy. It's a pure kiss. I can't understand it. The end is that I call to him:

"Little boy, little boy in white, little boy."

But he doesn't hear me. He goes and I wake up. I dream that dream every once in awhile. I wish someone would interpret it for me. I don't believe death comes like that, as a child, in white. Death comes . . .

There was no true actress there. She tried hard but in vain. I don't know if it's because I've seen a lot of theater on stages in other places, but for what she was, to be frank, Rachel was a fine looking woman, not an artist. When all that was going on, we were involved in the whole matter of books, long discussions in the cafes, and we spent all our time at the opera, and serious theater. We saw Caruso, Francesca Bellini's pictures, Tita Rufo, all the most brilliant things. You'd go to the Alhambra to have a good time with the lubrico-burlesque as Benavente used to say.

Nonetheless, I never thought of it as theater in the sense of dramatic work. Rachel was very pretty, but she always seemed to me to be half crazy. One time, in the '20's, she did a piece, if memory serves, written especially for her. Hers was the lead role and she played a woman who had gone crazy and drank to excess because her infant girl had died.

It was what Galarraga and that whole pantheon of writers called a tragic comedy. The crazy lady would come out wearing black robes, open her arms, begin to babble and put a bottle of rum to her lips. She paced alone up and down the stage, stumbling about and grumbling. Then she'd describe what she was seeing, like a review: little wooden horses, bats, a large ship, lots of red and yellow flowers, and that was the monologue Rachel would do night after night. It was a great success with the audience, that's the absolute truth. But even so. It always seemed to me to be a farce. She was herself when she was the vamp, the rascal, the femme fatale, I could never stomach her in serious roles.

Now, if left to Federico, he would have made her a Sara Bernhardt. Or am I being too critical?

Between Federico, my old lady, and the theater, politics had to be shoved at me. My old lady was a litany: "La Chambelona, Menocal, the death of so and so or peg leg . . . Girl, take care 'cause there are some nasty folks in that pig sty. Don't neglect to vote in the elections. Don't talk about what doesn't pertain to you. Don't get entangled. Ay, Grau, what a saint you are," and so on. Federico the same thing: "Love, you follow my lead in political matters. Smile at this senator or that one. Don't overdo yourself in social satires," and the theater which in the '20s was something like an anteroom for politicos. . . I had to be shoved into that whirlpool to learn everything about political life in Cuba. I can talk a bit but with no details. Whatever I might tell about is on the surface. Politics got to me but it was never the passion of my life.

I say that a woman in politics is like a man in the kitchen. You lose the genuineness of your sex, you become transformed, not into yourself. A woman's chores should be different: the house, love for her man, art, playing the piano, knowing how to make candy, to embroider, to be friendly, that is a woman. I haven't much followed these . . . how should I say, traditions, because my character was always different. I'm a little masculine in the good sense of the word. If I could have been an aviator I would have done it with pleasure. To jump with a parachute from 15,000 meters, to feel that emptiness and then touch earth. That was a dream I've never been able to see fulfilled. I know it is a man's mission, but it captivates me. Once I went to the movies for a whole week, to the No-Do, the Adventure News, to see a little tiny woman, who seemed like a jockey, jump with a parachute while reading a book.

Nowadays, politics is cruder; grudges, vengeance, hate between parties. If politics were honest and straightforward, maybe I'd have been a governor or something like that. But I always saw complications and distanced myself. In the Alhambra I did my satirical sort of plays, I tangled with senators, mayors, presidents, but it was a joke, with a dose of trouble making, but always in jest.

Politics has always overwhelmed us. We're condemned to draw blood. Cuba's people are an abject people, with a tragic disposition but a happy character. That's why in the theater we covered everything. We made fun of the politicians, of their wives, Mrs. So and So and Mrs. What's Her Name. They were all "pearls," the stupidest women, who got to be first ladies without knowing a single language that wasn't their own, and that poorly. Mrs. Záyas came from the Colon section and was the most democratic. Mrs. Grau was his mistress for many years, cuckolded his brother to get to the Presidency. When she came out of the Palace they threw a bucket of water on her and for the first time she was heard to say, from her car, "queers, bastards." The whole world knows about Mrs. Prío who was called the inkwell because anyone who wanted to could go and dip. And she suffered from an illness where people grow and grow depending on how much damage they do, that was her sickness.

If I had been the first lady of this country, I swear, the first thing I would have done is stand on the balcony of the Palace, grab a microphone and start to call to people: "You, what do you want? And you?" And like that, I would have ruined the Republic but nobody was going to be without help. I was going to fill the pockets of the man who'd lost an arm, of the paralyzed man, of the starving one, of all of them, with the country's treasury, because I don't believe in little parks, or in great buildings, let each person do what he wishes with his money, pay for his own illnesses, his ailments.

I surely wouldn't have lasted more than three days in the Presidency, but how good I would have felt and what a happy memory they would have kept of me. That would have been me as First Lady.

In the Alhambra I often got even. I invented little fibs to besmirch the politicos and avenge myself. The times were already heated up and you had to take care not to fall into a trap. The whole country was all stirred up.

Lots of money on the street, for the rich, and lots of hunger for the poor. The theaters were crammed full. The ones who went were the ones who could put their hands down into their pockets. The ones who couldn't, had to lick their chops.

Havana was always an appropriate space for spectacles. I couldn't see much, because of my job. But I did meet the big ones, I rubbed shoulders with them. None of that just seeing them close up. I mingled with them. For example, Caruso, I exchanged greetings with him one night in the doorway of the National Theater. I didn't manage to say anything to him. We only looked at each other. I understood all of it, but he was very old. He had fat little hands. Caruso was the nightingale of the world. Afterwards nothing better has come along in his genre. The envy of the delinquent element made him suffer a great embarrassment in Cuba, the poor man. He sang beautifully, even though he hit a sour note here in *I Pagliacci* and the people whistled him. It was a chicken coop, because I was there that night. I applauded with all my soul for the efforts made by that privileged voice which couldn't be human because it reached a supernatural register and vibrated like a cherub's.

Caruso cried in Cuba and all Cuba cried with him. That's how sentimental the country is. Later, to top it all, a bomb was placed near him, and the great divo, the top voice in the world, dressed as a clown or a prince I don't know which, took off running all the way down Prado. He ran from fright, as if the seat of his pants had been set afire with potash. What developed there was a big hubbub. The women pulling their hair and the men choking . . . Caruso didn't deserve that. He was removed from politics. And in those years Menocal was the gendarme here. People complained a lot. But the bomb scare, nobody could have avoided that.

That was what Bernhardt referred to when she called us savages in tuxes. We're very elegant for some things, yes sir, very delicate, but for a juicy role like that we're priceless. Some of us performers went to apologize, which he was grateful for because he was a simple, noble man.

Those kinds of things happen in politics. Whoever gets involved gets his hands dirty. Whoever doesn't get involved is defenseless. During those years you had to get on the teeter totter. That is, a little bump up and another one down. If not, a girl could lose her life which, for the little bit it lasts, I'm not going to say it's worth the teeter totter. The sad thing is to be banished by yourself, like many who started, because they lived with a senator or an advisor, voted, defended the president as if he were the Pope, and when things would get tough, there the poor little girl would go to ask for help. What one of them, who had already been a headline figure, asked for was to work as a chorus girl. Some women, how stupid! If they'd had a little more natural intelligence they wouldn't have stumbled so much.

Those kinds of things happen in politics. The just pay for sinners. And those women were the victims of tigers, dressed in white, with a straw hat, a red ebony cane, silver cuff links, the gift of gab, but tigers. That's why I stayed far from them. When one came to offer me the world the first thing I did was adjust my neckline. And if I could, I turned my back on them. I never wanted to get involved with that type of man.

I accepted gifts, of course, but the ones that came anonymously. When they'd bring the little card with the name of the generous one the next day, I was insulted and tore it to shreds. That way no one could accuse me of knowing my admirer. And all that because they dragged behind them the phantom of politics.

When the new currency was introduced, things got black. Some died of heart attacks, the soft-hearted ones and others were left speechless for the rest of their days. It was a very big "shock" for the Cuban man. I remember the sad faces of the millionaires. Havana empty, alone. A plague of grief fell on us.

In the Alhambra we premiered a play that talked about that . . . Lovely curtains made of coins, treasure boxes, dollar signs, the set was a veritable coliseum. And the bank of lights? Oh, what can I say about the shades: blue, lilac, mauve, magenta, orange, green, ochre for the beach scenes. The set of a real coliseum. I came out in the color of silver. Me as a beach bum. That role fit me like a glove. It was light and strong at the same time. I pulled my hair back, put on a pair of pants full of patches and holes in the knees and so on, to make trouble. On stage, I felt like an authentic bum. Without saying a single word I brought the audience to an ovation. The bum, dressed in silver, ran along the breakwater with a basket of fish in his hand and when he passed a citizen he pestered him shouting in his ear: "Look friend, gentleman, sir, here I have swordfish, red snapper, triggerfish, grouper, flying fish, sea bass, mullet, tuna, moray, sea robin, flounder, cod, herring, twenty kinds of sardines, delicious bluefish, so if you want some, let me know, 'cause I'll make you a portion right now . . ." Then the little colored boy Acebal, who was my street sidekick, would arrive, and he'd make me repeat the monologue and each time I'd mention more and more fish until it got to one hundred names said that way, by rote.

At the end, the audience sent me bravos and I had to repeat it up to six times. I finished hoarse and tired.

Like politicians, we always used jokes and ridicule, the Cuban's two lifesavers, for navigating in life.

Acebal, black as asphalt, had the soul of an angel, you could say. We became friends because we were compatible in many things. In the discussions about work, he and I were like one single voice. The others didn't say boo, because what was an illiterate girl going to say? Nevertheless, Acebal and I would add our spark in the meetings as often as we could. They always listened to us, above all to me who even without a university education, knew the psychology of my audience better than a professor.

I would give anything if you all could meet Acebal, the little colored boy Acebal. If he were sitting here now in that arm chair, we'd be laughing all night long, because he was a man who had some terribly witty thoughts. What Federico never had. Though very talented, he was a hard, dry man, with no spice.

Ay, old Acebal, wait for me, we're falling like little lead soldiers.

I was at that party. As a stock player, as a singer, as a dancer, as a blackface. Mostly in blackface. I played the Negro who would make me stand out. The nice black boy, the happy one, the crazy one, the one who would let himself get hit when it suited him:

"Acebal, bring the car around. Acebal, get this little stain out of the suit. Acebal, I told you to get the stain out," and fwosh, a shove and the black boy's on the floor. Nothing, just a character with social and political value. The Negroes, in my opinion as a white, are different. They move more like big dolls than like men of flesh and bone. They have an earthy kind of humor.

It was that spirit I tried to give the audience, the true spirit of the Negro: frivolities and eccentricities. The Negro has never suffered what the white man has, because he's been more a party lover and things that happen don't cause him any injury. All you have to do is see how given they are to music and dance. They're the kings of music, and I recognize that in them. Better than anyone else I know what a Negro is. Better than anybody, because I was such a catalyst for their characteristics that I could later earn my living playing them. I was the most popular Negro in Cuba, in spite of my white skin. Those are the paradoxes in the destiny of a man.

The colored race always viewed me as an ambassador,
they treated me like a king because they knew I had
fashioned an exact likeness of their idiosyncrasies.

Once they honored me in a social club known its morality.
The speaker cited me as an example, and surrounded by Negro
men and women, I became emotional and my eyes even misted
up. Those were the grateful people and not the ones with
rotted brains, like so many, like the one who insulted me once
on Apodaca Street, a colored ruffian, from the depths of
vagrancy.

The Negro sees me and shouts:

"Listen here, you little patent leather boy, with a
country hat, we're going to knife you to pieces when you least
expect it, for being a clown and a cartoon figure. You hear me,
we're going to . . !"

All of that because what they wanted was for me to bring
the refined colored, or the natural one, I don't know, to the
stage of our theater. In those years it was impossible. A
Negro with schooling was rare, and the same for a colored
orator, never mind a politician, so then, what were we going
to do?

We had to play the conceited Negro, the big daddy, the
scoundrel.

A handkerchief around the waist, preferably red,
another around the neck, a good knife with a thin blade, a
little straw hat, white teeth like coconut meat, that was the
Alhambra Negro.

In those times it was impossible to put the refined or
natural colored man on stage. I don't know, even today . . .

Acebal was a boy who had been raised in a poor
neighborhood, like me, why deny it? Like Adolfo too, may
God keep him!

So he knew more about the Cuban people than just
anybody. He was the one who took me by the hand to the
tenements, to the public schools, to all those places where I

could learn something about my people, their conversations, the atmosphere, the gestures.

"Notice how that Negress walks. Look at how that mulatta dresses, look carefully: coral tree beads, rings, taffeta. Red, Rachel, red predominates. Listen to what those two are talking about."

That was my friend, Acebal. A sponge made into a person. To do all that, to mix with the common folk, you have to be like them, very uncomplicated and fun loving. The Negroes and the Chinese aren't so easy to study. The Negro out of insolence and the Chinese out of distrust and pride. Like trunks, they hold it all in.

The Negro is dangerous. You have to approach him with tact. I won them over. I know it's a delicate topic. They went there, yes. Stage hands, cleaning boys, doormen, ice cream vendors . . . I've always dealt with all of them: Negroes, mulattos, octoroons, Chinese, whites . . . I've been a liberal and democratic person on that point. I've never liked discriminating against anyone, not even on account of color. How many times did they call me a pig for talking right in my doorway with a colored person! But me, like someone from Lima, what went in one ear went out the other. One night I set out with my husband to stroll through the harbor. It was very nice and cool and you could hear a military band in the distance. The music came from behind the Castillo de la Fuerza. We approached and in the Plaza de Armas discovered the clamor. It was a political speech, but a very elegant Negro dressed in white all the way to his feet was giving it. Around that time a Negro speaker seemed out of place. My husband, who was political and liberal like me, asked me to go with him right up under the nose of the aforementioned. It was a pleasure to hear him declaim in well learned diction, without hems and haws, with clear s's and even a sonorous voice appropriate for a stage professional. The Negro boy spoke about rural education, about the sewer system, and all was going quite well until a little turd let loose a Bronx cheer. I stood up and shouted: "Insolent hog!"

The Negro, thinking I was directing those insults at him, stopped speaking and was scared off that platform. He turned as green as an avocado.

I still think of that incident with deep regret. The truth is that it cut my soul because the man with his color and all was educated and had good intentions, the best. That's why I say that the issue of Negroes in this country is a delicate one. Very delicate. Right there, in the dressing rooms, I had unforgettable fights with my compañeras, because as often as they slept with Negro ball players, journalists, senators, Negro advisors, then they'd say that out of a nose as broad as a glove couldn't come a single idea. That's unfair and seems contemptible to me because a nose can't define a human being of flesh and blood who has a brain. I think the solution is that the Negroes stay Negro and the whites white. Each one in their just and human place, without unnecessary mixing. I've had colored maids, manicurists, Negro chauffeurs, cooks, and I've gotten along well with all of them. Me here, in my place, and they in theirs. That's the most appropriate solution. But who listens to me? Who comes to my house to ask for my advice? No one, because people here are already like the blind and deaf. That's why we're going to end up devouring each other sooner or later.

The walls of the restroom were full of drawings and writings and there were little flowers and someone even painted a grouping of little stags, perhaps because it suggested horns and it was a theater for hommes seuls.

The fact is that all Havana's cocottes had their great mural there, with names and addresses "How much Dangerous Anita? How much for a night Margot Swallowsitall?"

101

Then it said two dollars or less and "Thank you, Gentlemen" in big letters, because those women of pleasure were high flyers.

I, who went there very little, have very hazy memories, but one thing I can't forget, maybe because of my dreams of being a painter, was the "Rubensian" figure of Rachel, pompous, plump, undistinguished, but devastatingly sensuous. Once she arrived alone—as was usual to see her in Havana— all alone, at the Acera del Louvre. As she approached, the people from the Acera found positions from which to contemplate that statue.

She arrives and sits at the shoe shine stand, very serious, and says to the little colored boy:

"Boy, I got all muddy crossing Neptune Street, could you shine my shoes?

He looks at her bewildered and starts to spit and polish, spit and polish, but his eyes kept going toward her legs. So acting all offended, she asks him:

"What, you've never seen my legs?"

"Yes, queen lady, but never up so close."

I've saved my complexion because I never let myself be made up by anybody. The only being who put his fingers on my face was Adolfo. The poor thing, he knew all the beauty secrets. He saved my features, my complexion, my arms. At my age any woman has wrinkles and is already shriveled up. Not I. I conserve myself intact. My thighs are still hard and my breasts likewise. I dye my hair because I don't like grey hair. But I'm not very grey either. I could leave my hair natural and I'd look good.

At the Alhambra they accused me—those whom God didn't bless—of being unkempt. They understood beauty to be jars of cream, boxes of powders, lipsticks, eyebrow pencils . . . A fictitious beauty. The man who went out with them would have to scrub them with an aluminum pad. Me, on the contrary, simplicity and naturalness. For me the secret was rose water. Adolfo taught me how to use it: you take a vial of rose water, mix it with real thick almond milk and aluminum sulfate. Then you shake it up and spread it on the parts that are prone to wrinkles and you let it dry, that's it. My friends from the old guard come to my house and they say to me:

"How lovely you are, Rachel. You really are the same."

And they aren't fooling me because that's what that mirror over there is for and I may be many things but blind I'm not.

I'm proud of myself. I've been able to preserve myself, without falling into exaggeration. A comedienne like me, who sometimes had to make herself up like a mulatta even three times a day, could easily have a face today like a ruddy apple, like the sole of a shoe.

Of course, I also invented my own makeup. I kept it a secret out of vengeance. I don't know who it was, it was probably the Mexican. One night witchcraft was thrown into my dressing room. When I saw it, I felt a jolt and my hair almost all fell out. Thanks to the doctors I saved it, if not I would be a bald woman at this point. Horrible! So when I discovered that to make myself up like a mulatta I didn't have to use pomades that burned my skin, I didn't say a thing. I got my six or seven corks, burned them, put on some little drops of glycerine and a little bit of beer. With that I made my preparation. And later, people: "How wonderful, how similar, give me the formula, Rachel." But me, always evading. Because if have one thing it's that in my kindness I'm grudging, I save up what they do to me. A century or two can pass and I won't forget those who tried to annihilate me, like I won't either, clearly, the good ones. For them I'll have a gesture of gratitude always.

Those who have made me happy in life, there aren't many, can come to my house and ask me for whatever they want. I'm a loyal friend. I pray for them daily. And those who have made my life impossible, two or three women and a man, they will not come around. They will never come here, into this house. They know who they fought with. It's so hard to know that two or three have wanted to see a person destroyed, who have done everything, tricks of the worst kind, sabotage, everything. In the end, the man should have been more open, less twisted. Life is short, you have to live it in harmony. Daydream. If not, we fail. That's my philosophy, quite cheap, I know, but used with good results. You have to enjoy the happy moments. It doesn't matter how. You have to conquer the spirit and, depending on the circumstances, push on. I trust what surrounds me, how things are going, what to do with myself, and I take control of myself. If I'm alone, I seek company. If I'm sad, I put on Spanish music. If I get sick, I cure myself and until I do cure myself I'm not at peace. I'm a pest in everything. When Eusebio, my only true love, died, I tried to commit suicide but everything came out all wrong and since then I haven't again found the courage. I wanted to disappear completely. So that nothing of me remained, not even the ash. I turned it over in my head and this is what happened. A chair in front of me, a not too thick rope, in front of the chair a bucket full of alcohol, and a lit candle hanging from a little string that joined up with the rope lying across a stick, so that when I let myself fall, the weight of my body would knock the candle into the bucket of alcohol and then two things would happen: I'd hang myself and the candle would turn me into nothing. I did it but it seems my neck was too fine because the rope didn't even scratch me and the candle went out before falling into the bucket.

Since that incident I've decided to live until my days are finished.

Mama knew an old Negress in Oriente who, according to her, spent her life saying:

"Children, don't waste time, the body of joy is skinny."

How true! I repeat that and I get goose bumps, look: "The body of joy is skinny."

I came in '18. And what the hell! From the very first day I really liked it here. I'm from La Coruña, a very pretty but cold land. I got on a fishing boat and came over here. The boat was the "The Niagara."

Havana was very gay then. We disembarked in Machina and I threw down two or three glasses of rum there with some guys from home who had also come as stowaways on the same boat. Afterward, we saw the consul, he gave us some papers, and we began to work hard on the wharf, carrying sacks of sugar and rice.

I moved to San Isidro. My entertainment consisted of whores and drink. I met Rachel's mother, already old, something like three months after my arrival, because I was arrested with her for a matter . . .

We were in the station for a few hours and then everybody to their own house. As we left, the old lady tried to put the blame for everything on me and she began with the scheming and said to me:

"Galleguito, I'm not having any more to do with you. Anybody who goes to bed with children . . ." and so on, but I kept mum. I was already accustomed to that. My life is not a bowl of cherries, are you kidding, my life attracts ants.

The old lady helped me get work, better work, because that wharf job left my sides and back all bruised.

The little girl didn't get along with me. I say little girl, but she was already a good-looking young lady and was working as a singer at the Alhambra. Have you all heard about the Alhambra?

Well, that's where the girl worked. You'd go and see her, very beautiful, she had a little Gallician face but with some color from here. I'd get together two or three coins and I'd go over there at night, with a couple of associates, to see the striptease.

Here you don't get those blues that are so common in my country. Havana was "cathouses" with parties, women, and lots and lots of alcohol. My lord, the pleasures I had in this country nobody can take away from me. Two or three of us would come out of the theater, we'd head for the Colón section, which is still called that but they've closed it all down now, and we'd screw every girl in sight. Not even Rachel! Not even Rachel escaped!

A little colored man was the one who merchandised the women. A certain Cari would do me for free every month. I'd already started to work in the cemetery and she had an ossuary there for her mother. So I didn't charge her anything for cleaning it up and all, but every month I'd go over there and I'd give her a jiggle. Cari lasted me three or four years. One day I went there and they told me she had died of a bad infection. I left like a shot. And I found another one. Everybody loved that barrio, for the banter of the women, as they say in La Coruña, and I who spent all my time in the Alhambra getting worked up would go straight there to relieve myself, if not I'd explode like a firecracker.

I respected the daughter, of course. She was my age, but I tended more toward the old one. Besides, the daughter turned out to be real sharp. She only went around with people with dough, you know, with dough and style.

That girl caused a furor here. She ought to look older than me, because she wasted herself, yeah, she wasted herself . . .

Chapter Six

I feel young. The storms have passed and I haven't felt them. Or I've forgotten them. Or it's probably because I was a privileged . . .

I had the honor of premiering *Automobile Delirium*, a lovely play that showed the commotion the arrival of automobiles caused in Havana, both coupes and convertibles. I also premiered *The Island of the Parrots*, *Arroyito Highway* and so on endlessly.

For me, as for any performer, those openings brought on a horrible state of nerves. I lost weight in a matter of days. Last minute rehearsals and squabbles are among the worst things that can happen to a human being. Before rehearsal I would take three sedatives to avoid fights with the wild beasts. Then, opening day, we were all so emotional that we didn't even speak to each other, nothing happened, only silence and expectation. An opening day is unforgettable. Much more so when you have some leading role. That whole day is different, or not. I know for me the theater was transformed. The curtains shone like new, the sets, scintillating, the people's faces, different, like expecting something to happen, something that was never announced.

There was . . . yes, there was a prompter older than 80 who didn't want to retire for anything in the world. Each time the theater had a premiere, he would come to my dressing room to give me flowers. He always brought a happiness that I have never seen in a younger person. The face of that little old man and those flowers were the greatest incentive to go out on stage. Just seeing him made my soul happy. Like when you're sad and you open a music box. The little old man, I can say, was in love with me, resigned to it. I never did tease him, but I didn't treat him coldly either. I played with him, joking around. That kind of kidding around in the wings that doesn't go anywhere, and I know, I've lived convinced of it, that he didn't expect any thing else.

One night, at the last, when the theater was going down hill, when the nudity began and the foul jokes, the old man died.

Acebal and I were doing a skit. I had forgotten a few lines and I approached the shell discreetly. I made signs to him, the usual ones, but I didn't hear a reply. I saw Acebal's eyes full of horror, enormous, and when I looked at the shell the old man was passed out or dead I don't know. His head was lying on this part of his arm and his hair falling forward.

Acebal and I kept on improvising. The words wouldn't come out for me. When the curtains closed I ran to touch the old man. Heavenly soul! He was already cold, frozen like a cup of shaved ice.

Afterward, two or three more plays premiered and I worked, but without that anticipation, without the little face of that old man and his flowers, so tender! Theater life is sad but you dress it in colors and it becomes something else.

If it weren't for this hand that doesn't work well for me, I'd write something about my life. Naturally it would be a surprise for all who knew me. Because I was going to describe the other side. Not the one that was known but the one I covered up. The side no one knew, not even my husbands.

I was going to tell about the bitterness. A woman who has lived . . . Yes, who has lived to satisfy the whims of others. Without love, which is the only thing that can't be missing in a person's life. That's how I've lived. That's why I dream now. Real dreams, I'm not an dreamy dreamer but a real dreamer. I dreamed some days ago about the hugest ocean across from my house. In the ocean there was a yellow mango and a little wooden house, floating. The mango was bigger than the house, it was enormous. I didn't see myself but I sensed that I was approaching the mango instead of the house, I kept on approaching and I continued seeing it bigger and bigger, until it was like a wall of . . . of mango. Strange, no? Well, I felt panicky, my jaw locked up and I couldn't move. No matter how much I shouted, "Ofelia, Ofelia," no one heard me. It seems I went back to sleep and saw the mango again. This time with a little Cuban flag stuck on top. I considered singing in the dream, I don't remember what, but I sang and the little flag disappeared.

After a while, I was in a military parade with the little flag in my hand. And they applauded me. A crowd applauded me.

In another dream, I'm going along a sandy path and when I come to a river I meet a naked young man who calls to me. And I sense I'm moving but when I get there, I don't know if when I get there or before, a terrible thing, I wake up. That dream is like the one about the child, it leaves me feeling bad.

I've been told that dreams have to do with the stars, that you dream according to your sign in the horoscope.

My sign is Aquarius, which is a strange sign. For two sided characters. I'm a woman with two faces on account of that planet called Saturn. I have the creative line. It starts here in the palm of my hand, goes through this whole area and stops, with a shower of stars, at my wrist. That's the artist's line. All the greats had it, Bertini, Duse, Caruso himself.

My star is the moon. When there is a full moon is when I get to be frantic, surly, I don't want to see anybody and I feel like . . .

On a full moon no one can put up with me. Once I scratched myself on stage and I bled for days on account of the full moon, which is what carries everything along and makes blood flow without stopping.

I recommend to whoever wants to do something successfully to do it under a full moon. For giving birth it's ideal, for planting a tree, for memorizing. It's the moment of fertility, I'd say.

My birth stones are opal and chalcedony, which I've never seen but I'm crazy to. I wonder what it's like?

We Aquarians have one big happiness and one big misfortune. The curious thing is that they go together, hand in hand. We're also very slippery like water, which is our element. We can knock down a world when the waters gush, but the world also falls on top of us and destroys us when the waters get damned up. I die inside thinking about that. Each time I set off to do something I remember my sign and I restrain myself, not much, but with some control. We Aquarians tend to give ourselves at first glance, a dangerous but horribly attractive thing for us.

We are generous and selfless. We love human peace and harmony. What else? Ah! We're altruistic, we would want everybody to know how to subtract, multiply, divide, how to get out of poverty. We never lack money. Well, my sign has lots of things but I think that the most important is that it's a sign that makes advances, not like Cancer, which destroys everything it touches.

My true love was a Cancer. And though it might be hard for me to recognize, it sunk me in a swamp. It goes without saying that I was the one to blame, because he never misled me. When I run into someone who is a Cancer, the crab, I remember my love and try not to confide in that person because the zodiac never makes a mistake. Cancer and Aquarius don't get along but they do love each other. They are two forces in opposition. I still love him, in spite of that fateful sign that led him to screw everything up, his throat slit, my virginity lost.

The world is ruled by the stars. The harmony of the earth is due to them. For that reason you have to know how to find affinities. An Aquarian and a Cancer are like oil and vinegar, they need each other but they repel one another. I'm proud of my zodiac sign. It's been a guide for my life, at least in its practical aspects, because I never found a Leo, who would have meant my happiness. But why ask so much of life? I'm content with what I've had. As a performer I did whatever struck my fancy. I also did what my fantasy asked of me and I'm not going to complain for lack of love. I have to recognize that I was despicable too and I made some people suffer a lot with my wickedness and disdain.

My mother told me one time—I remember it was in the dressing room and she said to me: "Girl, what you just did is bad." And it was bad. I pulled the wig off of the Mexican right there on stage because she came up to me and instead of saying what she should have she whispered in my ear:

"Bitch, you're upstaging me."

The audience realized the woman had offended me and out of revenge and pride I yanked her wig off.

Later Mama came and reminded me that I had been born on a terrible day. The coldest day there has ever been in this country and the only one on which Havana was inundated by a tidal wave, causing disasters that have left horrible scars. Besides, that day there was an earthquake in Santiago de Cuba and the homes of two families collapsed, with the death of women and children.

That's why I pray when my birthday approaches. To Marianita and to Santa Barbara who have always been with me there, at the foot of my bed.

I had this prayer stuck up on my dressing room door for years. If I go out on the street I carry it in my purse and when I return home I put it under those glasses of fresh water. It's a prayer against the evils and for scaring away my enemies.

To say it you have to make 13 crosses with holy water on your forehead and say two or three Our Fathers:

"Oh, Virgin, keep these wicked, envious, fierce beings who lie in wait for me far away. I resort to you, Santa Barbara, so you can confuse them. You, sublime protector and generous Christian, who opens your heart for good beings. I enter there and I will come from there with the blood of your heart to liberate me from them and you will not allow them to interrupt my Christian march and, if they persist, you will send them headfirst to hell as a punishment for their wickedness and liberate me from all evil."

Amen. Amen. Amen. (I have to say it three times.)

The woman who came in and read that knew that she wouldn't be able to find my weak point. I'm protected until the day of my death by my sign and by my two saints, Mariana and Barbara. And I don't have to make petitions or put plantains under a ceiba tree, none of that.

It's enough for me to invoke my protectresses with my faith, with my voice, so that they hear me right away. Every time I had a quarrel with the Mexican I would shut myself up in the dressing room, not to hide from her, but to pray. I prayed a little: "Ay, Santa Barbara, don't let that snake in, don't let her in." Then you could hear the sound of high heels, the forcing of the door, and I prayed, I concentrated even more, and she went away on her own. Up to now it's been like that. Let me knock on wood just in case.

"You don't believe me, Ofelia, you don't believe me."

"Yes I do believe you, Ma'am, but it's that you repeat the same thing to me so many times that I don't know what to say to you."

"You don't have to say anything to me. I tell it to you because it's true, damn it. When have you heard me telling a lie?"

"I haven't said you lie. What I have said to you is that you spend the day with that same old song and . . ."

"But you don't want to hear. Is it that you're upset with me? Have I done anything to you, tell me. Because I believe that I couldn't have been nicer to you. You're not a maid here, you're one of the family."

"Well, I do come to work because you pay me. Isn't that so?"

"But it isn't the money. Let's not get into that. The treatment you've received here. The only one who dresses me is you, the only one who speaks on the phone is you, the only one with authority . . ."

"Ma'am, has that trouble with your back gone away?"

"It hurts less now. He hasn't called today?"

"No."

"Yesterday he called and he said today to wait for the call at four. He'll call at four."

"It's six, Ma'am."

"Then he called and we haven't heard it ring. You're deaf, Ofelia."

"I am not deaf. The phone *didn't* ring."

"He called at four but you're deaf."

"I am not deaf."

"Shut up already, shit, I'm fed up with you. You won't even talk on the telephone. How much effort can it be, Ofelia? Tell me, tell me."

"Don't raise your voice at me. Don't raise your voice at me."

"Come, move my bed for me, for God's sake. I can't do it by myself."

I have a head full of dreams. I've suffered from that affliction all my life. Sometimes I end up without any understanding, with a sort of emptiness . . . Ofelia is the one who knows me. It's not memory, no, even though she says it is, and she's bought me some little vials of stimulants. I believe it's thinking, dwelling on things. One time I went to the baths at San Diego and the waters there did me a lot of good. They're sulfurous and it appears that aids the nerves. I returned a new person. I have to go back. I've been very daring, very heroic, I've applied myself to crazy schemes. Life has been complicated for me, that's also why I've found

113

myself in just any old kind of situation, in all sorts of messes
. . . I've never been, what would I say, stuck in anything for
very long, never. More like a satellite wandering around out
of orbit. That's why my love affairs didn't work out.

The only place I felt good was in the theater and at that
for a season. And now in my house, though I need to have a
companion. Outside I've done many rash things. I like
adventure, and I always liked it. Because of my crazy ideas I
almost had Federico commit suicide. During Machado's
regime, it was in vogue to have a pleasure boat, a yacht. We
had one with the name of "Rachel I," Federico's idea! We
anchored at the Almendares wharf. I loved my boat . . . I got
my license and was the first woman skipper in Cuba. We'd
cast off, pull up the anchor, and out to Cayo Sol with a good
tide because in stormy weather, it was dangerous to go out.
But the sea makes you reflect. It's like a psychiatrist's office.
There, on one of those outings was when that monstrosity
came to mind. Young people's notions. He and I never got along
very well. He was obliging but syrupy and cold at the same
time. I don't know how to explain it. A character for women
with a lot of endurance.

I was and am a female and I needed, when he couldn't
give it to me, a real man. So one day I proposed an idea to him
that I'd been turning over in my mind. A crazy idea but a good
one to finish off a relationship, like with a gold brooch.

I acted desperate, neurotic, and asked for some pills. He
came to the bed with a glass of water and put a sedative in
my mouth. Then I asked him to sit at my side. He sat down
and I said to him:

"Federico, I want to die. I can't stand any more. If you
want we'll go together and that way it'll all be over. We
don't have to leave any traces. That's it, if you want. I've
made up my mind."

He answered me resigned, as if he'd been waiting for that
proposition of mine. It surprised me a little and all of sudden I
got scared. But I couldn't turn back, I couldn't.

The only thing he did was to take off his glasses and look at me.

"Rachel, what about the theater? Do you believe it's worth it to leave it?"

I started to cry and I think I slapped him.

"Then that cheap little theater is worth more than I am!"

Of course he didn't say any more. He took some pills and asked me to let him rest an hour. That night we had an invitation for a costume ball in the Tacón Theater. Those splendid dances.

We both went dressed in hooded cloaks. I was the happy one, he tried to pretend, but his eyes were popping out of his face. We were going to enjoy ourselves drinking and dancing. It was our last opportunity to see our supporters up close and to say goodbye to the world. We went for that reason.

We danced until three in the morning. That was to be our last night because from there we were going to go home to poison ourselves. I sang "Quiéreme mucho" at the party. They introduced me as the Belle of the Alhambra and the name stuck with me for the rest of my days. I took some hydrangeas that were on a carving table and I kept them in my bag.

I said: "The last flowers I will smell."

Federico didn't take his eyes off of me. Maybe he thought that idea was an illusion of mine and that it would slip away. But stubborn me. I didn't want to get drunk so as to not lose my judgement. He didn't drink either. I found him strange. He would come up to me and not say a word. He was a ghost of a person. He tried to soften me up but I resisted him. I persisted in my proposition, my guilty, idealistic, insane idea. The Tacón Theater was a gem. It had a very lovely paradise: angels, pale seraphim—all in pastels—and the hand of God trying to grasp the world. I began to look up, to contemplate the paradise, when I sense that a daring man, one of those you get at masked balls, is feeling my bottom. I've always had a good deal of behind and the guy seemed to be lecherous. He touched me and I gave a shout, frightened.

With that I heard a dry sound in the air. And I saw that my husband had the man in his grip, their two masks on the floor.

Not a second passed and the police arrived. We ended up the three of us in the Monserrate station house. We spent the night there in our hood and suffocating from the heat.

In the morning we left cleared of the charges. They released me at five. Federico and the man had to undergo questioning. I arrived at my house, washed my face and threw myself on the bed to cry. That fantasy, that dream of mine, wasn't able to be realized. It was frustrated by a vulgarity.

When Federico came and saw me crying he said to me:

"I understand you, my love, try to pull yourself together."

And he started to kiss me and that's when I felt a terrible disgust for the first time.

Mama wasn't fond of disputes nor did she like to see me suffer. She was life and happiness. She accused me of being crazy, of being absent-minded. I wasn't at all crazy, perhaps I have been absent-minded. Not crazy. But Mama, with that practical sense that saw everything, who even knew how milk gets inside coconuts and who you couldn't convince, was the first to counsel me to be free like a sparrow. I left Federico on her account. I didn't leave him suddenly. I went stretching out our contacts and loosening myself up inside. I checked my own conscience. He is good, but he's already too old and I have to live, he helps me, true, but I have my savings, and in that way, throwing one thing with another, I decided not to continue with the indecision. I wanted to fall in love in those months, to forget, to have a good reason and be able to tell him with all my soul: "Look, old man, you've been everything to me, but here is So and So and then there's this and there's that."

But no one with enough to offer came into my life. And I had to do it, like I say, coldly.

The Alhambra was already boring me. The Machado regime made that theater into a hell, like the whole country. I felt I was stuck in a hole without being able to lift my head up. It was the sensation of terror, a boiling cauldron. That wasn't politics. It was a war between brothers.

What happened to the Alhambra was what happens when you give parsley to a parrot. Since you couldn't let loose, it was sad to get there, say two or three little jokes and not do things freely. And I felt a bit like that myself because of Federico. My life was in decay. For that reason I had to leave him and begin to see the horizon again.

My fame didn't diminish but my audience liked to hear me do satire. I used to do the bandit, the vamp, the grand dame of society and those years muffled me. Me and all the others. I say that without getting into politics, venting a personal opinion. Federico, on the other hand, attempted to close me in. He'd say to me:

"Rachel, I'm going to buy you a piano so you can devote yourself to the concert."

I knew some pieces. I played the waltz "Over the Waves," Anckermann's songs, "If I ever kiss you," but the concert hall, no way! I no longer had a head for concert music. And I wasn't in love either. Maybe in love I could have dedicated myself to being a concert pianist. But at the side of that man, never.

I continued at the Alhambra, which was my life.

The piano and the concerts were the results of jealousy. He sensed that I no longer loved him.

Mama asked him to leave the house one night, to try it out. And he came back like a timid little rabbit. It pained me so much that I gave him a kiss and insulted my beloved mother. The poor thing, afterwards she didn't try to get involved in my business any more, and rightly so.

It was impossible already. I couldn't stand him. How horrible that is, what a prison!

117

One afternoon, in '26, we went to the horse races to gamble. My arrival there was an event. The journalists recognized me and immediately burned my eyes up with flash bulbs. More spirited, that day I wore a tailored suit, from Saxony, a material known as beehive, sky grey in color. My hat, precious, with a swept wing and crepe flowers around the crown and an abundance of bird of paradise plumes. I was, modesty aside, the most attractive woman there. Upper class women were never able to outdo me. I was up-to-date in fashion. Over there I still have the French and English magazines, which weren't popular here. The Cuban woman is voluptuous and the English woman, a stiff governess, the other side of the coin.

Well, we arrived at the race track by ourselves. We didn't speak the entire way. In my heart of hearts I hoped to meet someone who would move me that afternoon. Real gentlemen frequented the race track, often alone, and I said to myself, maybe . . .

The races don't fill me with enthusiasm. The exciting thing is the betting. My husband had the reputation of being a loser. Of course, he'd get there, wouldn't speak to anybody, would become block-headed . . . He had to lose for lack of spirit. Nevertheless, I arrived that day with the idea of being happy, and I proposed to myself to win. A second before my husband's horse was off, I stood up and began to shout. Me alone shouting.

"Get up, c'mon, get the dust out, now, you devil, stick out that neck, grab . . !

That was me. I stirred the men up. My husband, since he was sort of an idiot, didn't say boo. What I do know is that the horse heard me because he got to the finish line sweating blood. When that man announced the winner, the audience turned to me, applauding. I threw them a kiss and I won a small trophy that I have here on my right.

"Ofelia, bring that little box."

Rachel at the Race Track

The woman seen here, with the distinguished man of letters beside her (this article was accompanied by a photograph of me and Federico), like the princesses of the "azure" tales, possesses the whiteness of daydream and the crimson of life.

She loves all that surrounds her, is apt to become enthused and awaken the hearts of others, whoever sees her smiles from the moment she looks them in the eye. Facing this exalted luminary of show business, I sense the sweet sympathy of souls, which is the most gentle flower of our inner garden.

Rachel is, besides, the charming star of one of my most sincere and talented friends.

So that the entrancing femininity this reporter feels is somewhat like the extension of family affections. How could my pen silence the ambrosial adjectives and the dithyrambs of nectar faced with that sensational beauty which today commands the Hippodrome to add equine fury, and to our jockeys, fierce equestrianism?

Welcome, to this Harlequin stage which is our Oriental Park, the most attractive woman of our theater, the most beautiful woman, who, like that remote city of Persepolis, holds out for me the beckoning name of MYSTERY.

Newspaper, (Anonymous). February, 1926

We left there with our pockets full. We went to celebrate, to take our victory to a popular dance hall. Federico asked me:

"What are you going to do with that money?"

I answered that the money wasn't mine and that I didn't think I'd do anything with it. We got home, and, to avoid him, I went to sleep in Mama's room. That was the end. I made him remove the clothes he had in the armoire, the books and the work table that looked terribly ugly in the hallway.

He cried like an abandoned child. But he had to leave using the same truck we moved in with. I closed the door on the balcony, lowered the blinds and began to play the piano in order not to think, not to think.

"Ma'am, drink your lemonade."

"Lemonade gives me acidity. Reach me the chocolates."

"The chocolates will give you more acidity."

"Good, no matter. Ofelia, turn on the radio to see what they're saying about the cyclone."

"Just in case, I had the windows nailed shut."

"Why so many precautions? Another little cyclone, how silly! If the one of '26 was to catch you, what would you have done, Ofelia?"

"I think I would have nailed myself to the wall."

"I've never known a more cowardly woman in my life. All that you've lost, girl."

"Ma'am, have you heard talk of flying saucers?"

"Look at what you come out with. Of course I've heard about flying saucers. Flying saucers are star space ships that peer at earth once in awhile and light up the whole planet with a very shiny white light, just like when you toss a new coin in the air at night. Also, they float and spin with some space handles controlled by the ones who live inside."

"Do you believe they're going to touch down on earth?"

"But Ofelia, what world do you live in? There have been lots of flying saucers on earth, touching down, threatening, capturing people and leaving some powders that later become ashes and holes in the ground, like that one that came, don't you remember, to the Rancho Boyeros Park. People saw it and then it left a tremendous hole in the ground covered with ashes."

"I feel terrified."

"Not me, because, in the end, life on earth isn't so good or worth so much grief. I wish they'd come in droves to get me, and take me in that ship to another planet in the universe, Venus or Mars, whatever, to be able to live other experiences and improve, because the truth is we're offered nothing here, people devour themselves, they hate each other, there's no peace, nothing. Yesterday, just yesterday, I heard an imbecile say that there was no life on Mars. They're crazy, because they want to know without books, without investigating. I know that they live over there like here, with an eye in their forehead, not eating or reading. They don't have to work. All is joy, lots of parties, no worry, strolls. I would give everything I have to live there, no matter how much they say there's no vegetation, and I love plants."

"Ma'am, I think you've gone too far."

"No, dear, it's that you don't climb out of your shell. You have to dream. If this life is everything, if it all ends at that, holy shit. I, at least, don't accept that. I want to go on living, on Mars, on Venus, wherever, wherever! But knowing that I'm not going to be around to be food for worms."

It smelled French, a smell of something that came from there. All of us smelled alike. It was the fashion, the delight in that exotic scent. Rachel was always very vain and refined. She was the one who sprinkled us with bottles of perfume.

She was a superficial character, that fit right in at the theater. The only real flapper among us.

Though there are people around, there have to be, who might say it smelled like a brothel there, I say no, not a touch of brothels, pure French, Arpége.

Decent families were represented in the front rows: Catholics, Masons, store owners, wealthy men, vain men and men of letters, there were so many, poets, journalists . . .

"There is no doubt, the President, and the Mayor of our prestigious city, without doubt, have agreed that this theater is the lively representation of our national art. The most faithful of our national stage. The cream and the top, yes sir. The cream. Many thanks."

And the Alhambra was already being invaded by termites. Between the Machado regime and the nudity, the theater was crumbling away. The plays had lost their humor. The government imposed a controlled theater—a gag in the mouth—something that didn't fit there. The doors were being eaten away, the curtains were falling down rotted, plagues of roaches and rats entered the dressing rooms and, to finish killing it off, the marquee came down bringing with it a piece of the facade. And there were injuries. That's why they closed it and it never opened again.

I didn't wait for the boards to fall on my head. I left before that. A couple of months before the collapse. I'd arrive there, to work, and it just wasn't the same. I'd get there disenchanted. Federico tried to destroy me and he stopped giving me the roles that suited me. He wanted . . . yes, that very spiteful person wanted me to do the old ladies, the institutional employees, tyrannical women with high collars, the chubby cheeked country lasses and the melodramatic ones. Since I've always been a cheerful woman that infuriated me. The result was that I became disillusioned with the world. And I beat it out of there.

I went back several times because I wanted to see the theater, the people going in and coming out, the gossip in the audience . . . I'd stand on the corner of Virtudes Street, next to a pawn shop that was there, and watch. To see from outside is different. You get a different impression. It's like the theater was an optical illusion. That's why I went so much. I'd put on worn out street clothes and mix with the clientele of the cafe across the street. People said I was needed there, that the theater wasn't the same, that I was the heart and soul, and all the things people say. I was going in order to give my farewell. When I abandon something, or leave someone or when I go to another place, I like to see it clearly, to carry it away etched in my memory. That's what I did with the Alhambra. If I hadn't done it I would be dying now.

One night I decided not to go anymore, nor to see the people, not anything. The next morning was when I cried a little but I pulled myself together and that's that.

The movie era was just beginning then in Cuba. I made my attempts to get in, but the vipers were so numerous that I left it to fortune.

I knew a district attorney from Matanzas, very well heeled, who had been repeating for some time:

"Leave the theater and I'll give you a monthly allowance of 1500 pesos."

I received that money for several years. 1500 pesos, without working, in my house, and with the memory of my public and my fame. What more was I going to ask of life? I did whatever I felt like. Now it was me alone in the world of my home, with Mama and my friend.

I bought seven two-story houses in Havana and rented them. Some young chicks just recently arrived from the country worked in one of them. They had a bar and a madam who was in charge of receiving the men. That assured my future. My husband never found out about that business. It was my official thing, not a public one, and I preferred never to tell him anything. He was a good man, he had his quirks, but he didn't fence me in.

I was a sparrow for the first time. Free in my house. The dream of my life. Free for my own activities with no professional engagements.

Months later the announcement of the demolition of the Alhambra appeared in the press. There went my life, more than twenty years dedicated to the theater, my best years.

Later, journalists started coming to my house, like they still do, and they ask me questions, and I tell them not to make a fantasy of all that, but they keep hammering on it and so I begin to tell about it. What choice did I have! For me, to remember is the greatest thing there is. A person without memories is just like a tree without leaves. And I don't forget anything, I can't. That's why I left Mama's room untouched. I pass by there and it seems I see her in bed. And, she's dead, I know, but to me she's living. Mama was my beacon. The one who showed me the road. She made me an artist with a decent career. She managed it with her temperament and for that one has to be grateful to her. To my mind, Mama lives in that room and in her crypt in the cemetery, like Adolfo. They stay with me even though they may no longer be here in the flesh.

I've experimented: "Mama, Mama," and I feel a fresh little breeze in my head. That's my mother. The same with Adolfo. I say to him: "Adolfo, Adolfo, brother of mine," like that, in a whisper, and it's the same breeze. So, how am I not going to believe they're at my side? I believe it and I feel it.

I've never cried for them. Since it was what I most wanted, the tears never come. I go almost every Tuesday to the cemetery because on a Tuesday Mama died and on another Tuesday Adolfo did. I take them flowers. I pray for a few hours and I'm calm there, at the tomb of the two of them, because they're together. Adolfo below and Mama above.

I've had to buy an awning so the noon sun doesn't hit me. The awning and some gardening shears so the rains don't catch me by surprise. When I see clouds in the sky — those heavy-leaden clouds—I open the shears and cut off the electricity. Then it doesn't rain. I learned that from my mother too, poor little thing, waiting down there for me. But I know that I've got a lot to travel yet.

At times I say: "Send yourself, send your own self," but nothing. Death doesn't come like that. She's spontaneous. She comes when it seems right to her. I'd like to die to music. To die happy. In short, I never was a dramatic person. I would like to lie down one night, put on a waltz and fall asleep peacefully.

I've told Ofelia that if I die like that to do my make-up right, make me pretty and put my mirror on my chest. A mirror to see my face. That's my dream. I'd like my public to remember me just as I was. But Ofelia doesn't pay any attention. She spends her life telling me: "Ma'am, you're going to outlast half the world." And I'm for believing her because I still feel full of life.

Return to the theater? Not that. But live, what you call living, that certainly.

I'm not prepared for death.